THE FALCON CHRONICLES: BOOK THREE

WILDS OF THE WOLF

Also by Steve Backshall

THE FALCON CHRONICLES: BOOK THREE

WILDS OF THE WOLF

STEVE BACKSHALL

Orion
Children's Books

First published in Great Britain in 2014
by Orion Children's Books
This paperback edition was first published in Great Britain in 2015
by Orion Children's Books
an imprint of Hachette Children's Group
Published by Hodder & Stoughton
Carmelite House
50 Victoria Embankment
London EC4Y 0DZ
An Hachette UK Company

1 3 5 7 9 10 8 6 4 2

A catalogue record for this book is available from the British Library

ISBN 978 1 4440 1088 6

Printed in Great Britain by Clays Ltd, St Ives plc

The paper and board used in this paperback are from well-managed forests
and other responsible sources.

www.orionchildrensbooks.co.uk

To my own Clan, my friends and family.

"We humans fear the beast within the wolf because we do not understand the beast within ourselves."

Gerald Hausman

An old Cherokee told his grandson about a battle that goes on inside us.

"My son" he said. "The battle is between two wolves inside us all.

"One is Evil – anger, envy, jealousy, sorrow, regret, greed, arrogance, self-pity, guilt, resentment, inferiority, lies, false pride, superiority, and ego.

"The other is Good – joy, peace, love, hope, serenity, humility, kindness, benevolence, empathy, generosity, truth, compassion and faith."

The grandson thought about this, then asked his grandfather: "Which wolf wins?"

The old Cherokee simply replied, "The one you feed."

Cherokee legend

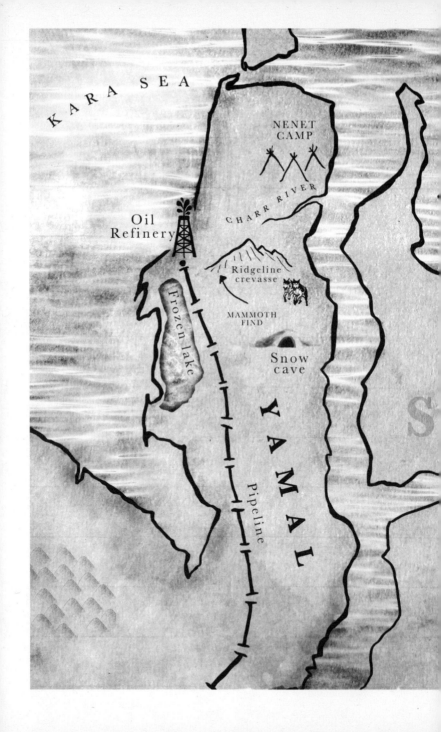

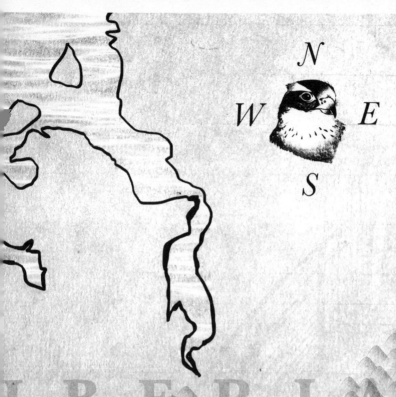

IBERIA

WILDS OF THE WOLF

ACTION. DANGER. ADVENTURE.

RUSSIA

PROLOGUE

Under soft footpads, the crunch of thin crust, from thawed then refrozen snow. These last few days have been too cold for fresh snowfall. Another crunch . . . careful. The wolf moves forward, letting his nostrils be his eyes. His muzzle drops to the ground and he fills his nasal cavities with delicious scents. Here in the dry, clear air of an Arctic winter, his canine nose sees the world in a kaleidoscope of odours; to him the air is as full of perfumes as a Turkish bazaar. Steam spume streams from his snout. It's well below zero and his breath explodes like smoke. Again he snorts, drawing in a faint, faded ammonia scent. An elk urinated here more than a moon ago.

A huge sniff, and a memory bursts like flame in his brain. A memory of spring. But it is just sweet chlorophyll from where the elk scraped and tore at grass stalks below the snow. Under the pale umbrella of a pine, the permafrost has been turned over by a squirrel, digging frantically to find its autumn nut horde. It didn't succeed and went hungry, the wolf notices.

He is a male of five summers, amber eyes electric against his gunmetal blue fur. He only took control of his small pack as the days shortened at the beginning of the winter. It had been a bold move for him to challenge the alpha male so soon. The old wolf who led the pack then was bigger and stronger. He had a massive ruff of fur about his neck like a lion's mane, and he was missing an eye; lost in a battle with a stag's pointed antlers.

When the younger wolf came to challenge the alpha, he used this weakness to his advantage, attacking constantly from One Eye's blind side. Gunmetal Blue tore at his underbelly and throat till he admitted defeat, and ran yelping; beaten, bloody, tail hugging his belly. His fate would be to wander the woods alone. Perhaps One Eye would starve, perhaps another elk would finish him off.

To be the alpha, you don't have to be the biggest, but you do have to be the canniest and wiliest. Gunmetal Blue was now the only wolf in the pack with the right to mate. It is a privilege and comes at a price. Wandering nomad wolves and lesser-ranking males will always seek his position, and he is responsible for feeding and protecting his pack. Now the harshest part of winter is over, and Gunmetal has passed the test of leading the pack through the days of endless darkness. But they're hungry. They've eaten no more than the odd snowshoe hare, and the pack

2

is eight strong. They need a large meal and soon, or there will be no pack left to command. He trots lightly on furry footpads, nose always to the ground, snuffling, urgent. What is that? Something sets fireworks off in his brain. He halts, as if frightened, to blow away any trace of the smell. The other members of the pack stiffen, heads raised as one, watching their leader.

Has he found something? A sniff again, in exactly the same spot. Blood! It's faint, not a smear left in the snow, but airborne droplets, carried on a breeze and dropped here. Faint, but fresh. The blood was sprayed, perhaps a sneeze from a bleeding nose, or bursting from a wound. The wolf begins coursing again, moving forwards, head swinging side to side with urgency. Nothing to the left, nothing in front, but to the right a couple more microscopic drops. He moves in the direction of the highest concentration of smell.

He is totally consumed, drunk with the rusty-iron perfume. The pack need to become his eyes and ears. As the trail grows intense, he sees a few drops of fresh blood stark against the white of the snow. Members of the dog family perceive things differently to humans. The structures in their eyes that give them night vision are better developed than ours, but those that discern colour are not as good. To Gunmetal, the blood looks oil-black against the snow.

Something is tugging at his brain, a deep intuition nagging, trying to become a thought. What is wrong? He lifts his head, alert, ears forward, satellite dishes directing sound towards his sensitive inner ears. A clump of snow drops from an over-weighted bough. An icicle creaks under its own weight. The earth breathes.

And then the thought forms. This blood is from a new kind of prey he does not recognise. It is not the elk that bellow in the autumn, or the caribou or reindeer who are guarded by dangerous humans. It"s neither rabbit nor beaver. It is too rich. It doesn't fit. Too late, he sees movement ahead, and a shape long, thin and too straight to be natural. There is a glint of a substance that is not ice. The same blue as his gunmetal fur. And in that second he makes out the shape of the human, kneeling, rifle ready.

Perhaps One-eye would have known. Maybe Gunmetal outwitted the wily older wolf too soon. This trap could take his whole pack.

Gunmetal Blue's decision is instinctive; defence through attack. As he leaps forward, the other members of the pack scatter. A crack, as violent as the collision when two musk oxen thunder head to head. The first bullet hits him in the shoulder, sending him somersaulting through the snow, clouds of white spiral like tornados. He gets straight to his feet and charges towards the threat – got to buy time, got to keep running. The second bullet hits him in the leg, splintering bone, bringing him down, yelping with pain. The human is standing, seeing that the other animals have fled, and his long wait has been all but wasted. Cautiously, the man walks towards the wolf. He knows predators are at their most dangerous when wounded. He slings his rifle over his shoulder, and takes a wooden club in his hand.

Despite his shattered leg, Blue stands. He sees his own blood spattered in the snow. Oil-black against perfect white. The blast has thrown him sideways, so he turns to face his enemy, hopping on his lame, useless leg. Another yelp, then he bares his teeth, a guttural snarl comes from his belly; "face me, leave my family".

Red-flecked drool drips from his mighty canine teeth. The hunter pauses. Perhaps he needs to shoot again? But the wolf stumbles, then lies down.

The last thing Gunmetal Blue sees, is leather boots approaching, crunch, crunch on the thin crust of thawed then refrozen snow.

1

A boy and girl walked in single file along a barely perceptible trail. Despite being in their early teens, they somehow seemed at home alone in the Arctic forest. The boy was in the lead, stopping every few minutes to crouch in the snow. He removed one thick woollen mitten, and pressed his pink fingertips into a footprint, tracing the shape of the toes, the claws, the heel pad. It was as if he was feeling for some warmth left behind by the animal they were following.

He looked up at the sky. Watery blue, with weak sunlight filtering through the suspended ice crystals of high cirrus clouds. The wispy mare's tails were the first signs of an approaching high-pressure system. "The weather's going to change," Saker said. "We need to make a good camp tonight."

Sinter didn't ask how he knew. He would tell her in good time, but while he was concentrating on tracking, she didn't want to distract him. Saker was volatile at the best of times, but when he was intent on following a trail it was as if he was in a trance. Their target animal had taken a path through the spindly trees of the taiga forest, thin Siberian spruce and larch trees drooping under their white load, like starving vagrants waiting in a soup-kitchen queue. It's no accident the trees are so slender. They have no time to grow. The Arctic summer lasts no more than a month or two, and even then night-time temperatures are freezing. Besides, broad boughs would collect too much snow, and collapse under the weight.

The local Nenet people called this remote Russian peninsula the Yamal. It means "The End of the World". Looking around, it was easy to see why.

Saker stopped so suddenly Sinter practically walked into him. He was silent, still staring at the prints in front of him. Sinter was about to ask him if he was all right, when he broke into delighted laughter.

"How about that!" he said. "I've been following this for hours, and never noticed till now!"

Sinter crept forward to see what he was looking at. In front of them the single deep track suddenly diverged, and an identical but much shallower trail of paw-prints branched out then came back to the main trail.

"What's happened? Has he stopped and doubled back or something?" Sinter asked.

"Well, that's just it," Saker replied. "There is no he. Or there might be, but not just one. We've been watching this trail like hawks, and I've only just noticed there's more than one animal. There could be five or six of them."

"Really?" she asked, surprised. "How does that work?"

"Look back at the marks we've made," Saker said. She looked behind her. There was only one set of footprints not two. They'd been walking single file, and she'd been putting her feet deliberately into his footsteps. It was easier that way; his feet had compressed the snow so she didn't sink so much.

"The wolves have been doing exactly what we do," Saker said. "It saves energy, and makes it much more difficult for other animals to assess how big the pack is. They're so canny!"

Sinter stared at the wolf tracks. It was all she could do to tell them apart from lynx, or Arctic fox, but Saker saw a whole complex story, as if he was reading a book.

"They're moving easily," Saker went on. "They certainly don't know they're being tracked. Look at this stride pattern, it's relaxed, they're in no hurry."

"If only they knew," Sinter said, looking down at the other set of prints alongside those of the animal track. Prints made by large leather boots.

Saker and Sinter had been following the animal tracks for two days before they'd seen the human prints, and realised they were not alone. The right kind of snow is the best medium for picking up and holding a track. If it gets too icy then the animal just skids about on top leaving no trace. Too soft, and the prints will be a mess and impossible to read. They had perfectly consolidated snow, exactly firm enough to take an imprint, as if it had been pressed into plaster of Paris.

It had been too cold to snow these last few days, which also worked in their favour, as otherwise the tracks would have been covered. The footprints stretched off into the woodland in an enticing manner, beckoning them, like a trail of breadcrumbs left behind by a child in a fairy-tale.

Sinter recalled how Saker had reacted when he'd discovered them. He'd turned into an over-excited bloodhound, and she'd felt she needed a leash to prevent him bolting down the path after them.

"Here, here!" he yelped. "The toes on his left foot are a little deeper than his right. Maybe he's injured." Sinter realised he was talking about the human prints now. And then, "No! He's carrying something over his left shoulder, so he's heavier on that side. And here, this is why!" He pointed to a line through waist-deep snow. "It's a rifle, being carried muzzle down, it's trailed through the snow."

He sprinted another hundred metres through the silent frozen wood, then stopped.

"And here he's gone down on one knee to look at the tracks. He stayed here for at least a minute." Saker brushed a few crumbs from the ground. "And he ate a cookie!" Now he was seeing the tracks so clearly that it was as if the man was walking right in front of them. Saker watched the ghost, seeing what he would do next.

"He sped up," Saker said. "He wants to be home before his wife puts dinner on the table!"

Sinter was bemused. All she could see for sure was that they were following a big man. He had big feet, and his prints were much deeper than her own, so he was certainly much heavier.

It had been nearly an hour, and still Saker trotted alongside the prints as quickly as he could push through the snow pack. However, Sinter noticed that his enthusiasm had faded. Instead his mood had become dark, brooding. Something in the tracks was troubling him. Eventually she couldn't keep quiet any longer.

"What is it Saker? Something's different isn't it?"

He stopped and frowned. For a second she thought he might snap at her, but instead he replied without looking at her. "I thought the wolves were too smart for him. I thought the hunter was just aimlessly following the tracks, and would never catch them. Now I'm not so sure."

"Why not?" Sinter asked.

"He's biding his time, never speeding up or wasting his energy. And he's taking shortcuts . . . it's as if he knows where the wolves will go. This isn't the first time he's been on their trail."

"But surely that won't work," she said, trying to soothe him. "The wolves here know to be cautious."

"They do," Saker responded. "And most of the year they range over big distances. You could never predict what they'll do or where they'll go. But it's different now. The winter's been hard, they're hungry, and they need to hunt. All their prey, the elk and deer are in the valleys where it's a bit warmer, and they can dig down to the grass under the snow. While the food is here, the wolves will be too, and they're keeping to fairly obvious trails."

Sinter nodded. That made perfect sense – well, as much as anything here made sense to her. She had spent her whole life in the constant embrace of tropical heat. This was the first time she had walked in snow. The bitter blast of a Siberian winter was a tough way to learn.

Saker continued. "If I can figure that out, then the hunter certainly can. He's planning an ambush."

Sinter's heart sank. It was less than a month ago that the two of them had been sitting in the rainforest, their laptop connected to the outside world by satellite link, and first learned of the horrors facing the Yamal peninsula. Their friend Minh had sent a series of emails and photos, detailing how black gold; natural gas and oil, had been found. All of a sudden billionaire businessmen were plundering the frozen frontier, and the native people and animals simply had nowhere to hide. As the outsiders came, the first animal they sought to destroy was the one they feared most; the wolf. Within a few years, they could be destroyed.

Saker and Sinter had made a pact to become a tight Clan, dedicated to making a difference. They hadn't yet settled on much of a plan. So far all they had was a vague idea to travel to Yamal, to get a sense of what was going on. When they figured out who was most guilty, they would deliver a carved wooden bullet as a warning. If the warning wasn't heeded, then they'd think about doing something more extreme.

It turned out the whole situation was more complicated than they'd anticipated. Wolves were being killed in huge numbers by hunters and local people, but also by rich businessmen, who would take time out while visiting the gas and oil fields, to head off on a snowmobile and shoot a few wolves for fun. Finding one person who could be held responsible was going to be half the battle. They'd decided to head to the main oil and gas refinery, and scope it out, but had picked up the trail of a good-sized wolf pack, and then the hunter's tracks.

Saker stiffened. Something was wrong. The wolves had suddenly spread out, they were no longer walking in each other's footprints and their steps were cautious. Perhaps they were about to start hunting.

"The alpha male has picked up a scent," Saker said. "Look here, his nose has made a little furrow as he sniffed the ground."

"But there's no sign of prey," Sinter said. She was right; there were no elk or caribou tracks, no places where deer had been nibbling bark or saplings.

"But there is blood," Saker stated, his voice thick with misery.

"So they made a kill?" Sinter asked hopefully.

"No." He breathed out and knelt in the snow again. "A wolf kill is unmistakable. The pack all feed together, they brace back with their forepaws – like this." He held his arms straight and down, mimicking the pose of a wolf feeding. "They tear their heads from side to side to rip out chunks of meat. What remains of the carcass looks as if someone's put a grenade into it and blown it up. There would be blood, fur, bits of bone everywhere, like a butcher's shop floor."

His voice shook. "This was much more clinical." He picked up a discarded shell casing. The snow around it had melted from the warmth of the bullet spat from the hunter's rifle. The simple piece of brass had grim significance. A wolf had died here.

"At least it was quick," Sinter said. The two of them had already seen the agony caused by leghold traps, and heard tales of wolves chewing their own legs off to escape the vice-like grip of those barbaric devices.

"The death was quick," Saker replied. "But the alpha male has been killed. The pack has no leader. They're starving, the last thing they need is to waste energy battling over who takes control . . ."

His last few words were drowned by the roar of a raging dragon in the treetops above their heads. Sinter dropped to the ground clasping her hands over her ears, as a blizzard whipped around them caused by the fierce downdraft of the behemoth flying overhead. Flurries bit into her cheeks and blinded her. From behind her fingers she could just make out Saker stumbling to his feet and sprinting as fast as the deep snow would allow him, towards the dragon as it flew off above the treetops. Saker broke out of the trees, finding himself at the top of a ridge-line. Below lay the broad expanse of a valley, surrounded by ominous-looking mountains. The huge Chinook helicopter that had just blasted its way over their heads bore off towards the horizon, the whop-whop-whop of its rotors slowly fading.

There at the meeting of land and sky was its destination. For days now, the only sign they'd seen of human beings was the one set of hunter's footprints. But far away on the plain was a tangled morass of concrete cooling towers, pylons spewing flame and smoke, vast grey buildings with helicopters and snowmobiles whining around them like mechanical gnats. It was as if someone had taken Batman's Gotham city, dumped it in the Siberian wastelands, then set it on fire.

Sinter came up alongside Saker, gasping at the chill of the wind-blown ice in her throat. She saw familiar steel forming in his dark eyes. She saw he had one pink hand free from its woollen mitten and was fingering something as if it was a sacred charm. Without looking, she knew it was a carved wooden bullet.

2

Sergei braced against the wind, dropping his chin into the snug collar of his parka. Within seconds his warm breath had started to dampen the fur, and he felt claustrophobic, so once more exposed his chapped lips to the air. He needed to breathe. Swinging his sledgehammer increased his breathing and heart rate, he needed to stay vigilant to make sure not to smash toes he couldn't feel.

Sergei was Moscow-born. He had seen plenty of icy winters, but not like this. This was an incessant, determined cold that had no end. If you left flesh exposed for even a few minutes it would quickly turn pink, red, then blue. Before you knew it, the skin would bear the waxy quality of early-stage frostbite. Leave it much longer and your flesh would burn black as if charred by flame, and fingers or toes would probably be lost.

He had to break chunks of ice out of his beard every

half an hour or so, and no hot tea or soup provided lasting warmth. He hated it. In the 20th Century, millions of Russians had been sent to the wastelands of Siberia, known as the Gulags, for speaking out against the political system. Many died there in appalling squalor. Sergei thought – not for the first time – that this job, stranded well within the Siberian Arctic Circle was much the same. The only difference was that bringing in black gold was lucrative work. He'd earn enough in six months to be able to live comfortably for the rest of the year.

Every morning his crew grumbled like work-shy donkeys over their breakfast hot oats, trying to put off the moment when they'd have to leave the warmth of their prefabricated plastic huts. But they were tough men, and once they were outside, the moaning would stop. They slammed their sledgehammers down on the iron rivets binding the sections of the huge oil pipe, only stopping to clap their hands together, to stimulate their fingertips. Most of his comrades were quiet during the day. Their minds far away with their families, thoughts of summer holidays by the Black Sea, and what they'd do with their windfall when this Siberian stint was over. These were good men Sergei smiled to himself. Men you could depend on.

His smile was abruptly broken, as a huge Chinook helicopter passed overhead. It was a retired military bird, still painted dark green with red Soviet stars. The occupants liked that hint of history and military might. However, Sergei knew that inside the Chinook was decked out to look like a luxury private jet, with plush carpets, leather sofas and huge televisions. The big money oilmen would make an appearance every few weeks, staying in purpose-built suites where they dined on steaks shipped in from Japan, and looked out at the bleakness of the oil operation from the sanctuary of a bubbling hot tub! When they came to inspect operations some wouldn't even use snowmobiles. Instead they'd come in centrally-heated buggies, peering through the windows at the workmen, as if they were some curiosity at the zoo. They had become fabulously, disgustingly wealthy from effectively stealing oil and gas from the people who really owned these lands.

The oil and gas fields that had been found under the Yamal peninsula were thought to be the biggest in the world. The pipeline that would carry the gas from Siberia across Europe would be 2600 miles long, and cost $5billion. More money than many whole countries made in a year. A few people were going to get absurdly rich from plundering Yamal. But it wouldn't be Sergei. And it certainly wouldn't be the Nenet tribesmen who had herded their caribou there for over a thousand years. Sergei slapped his face to bring some feeling back to his cheeks, and swung his sledgehammer down onto already rusting metal.

There was one man in particular who they'd all instantly hated. Even here, where everyone was clad in a dozen layers of clothing, he dressed in a fine suit and hand-stitched leather boots. If he ever wanted to get out of the vehicle, the driver would lay a carpet down to prevent the leather of his boots from staining. He was always tanned, as if his skin had been painted with creosote. Just to complete the picture, he wore a cowboy hat and string tie. "The American." Sergei would practically spit as he approached. At least for the most part in the Yamal, rich Russians were stealing from poor Russians. But the idea of a foreigner coming in and taking their nation's black gold. That was too much for them to stomach.

Saker and Sinter were still a hundred metres away when the dogs heard them and took voice. They'd left the ten huskies loosely tied to the sled that morning. The dogs had fussed, yipped, yapped and quarrelled for a few minutes while the blood still coursed warm round their bodies. However, as soon as they'd cooled down a little, and realised there would be no more running for a while, they quietened, walked round and round in the snow to pack themselves a bed, and lay down. The small hollows they formed would be enough to shelter them from the wind, their thick coats would keep them insulated, and like an Arctic fox they could cover their sensitive eyes and nose with their tails. They'd lie like that until they got painfully hungry, or until they heard their owners. Now they sensed Saker and Sinter's return they suddenly became aware of their hunger. They leapt and strained at their leashes, their barking as high-pitched as eager puppies, greeting the young humans as if they'd been away for months.

Saker and Sinter knew they were supposed to stay aloof from the dogs, showing no affection, and only interacting with them to give discipline. The Russian they'd bought the team from told them this was essential; "a good team of dogs is like a pack of wolves," he had said. "Every dog is just a few good meals away from being a wolf, the wild hides in the mind of every good Siberian husky and it is what makes them good. As a wolf pack works together to hunt elk, so your team of huskies work together to pull your sled."

The Russian had taught them which dogs took on which roles, how to run them, how to hitch them to the sled, and how to steer them across the most challenging terrain on earth.

"Let them know you are their leader," he had said. "You do them no favours by being kind. You must be the alpha of their pack. This is the only language they understand. If they find you strong, they will drag your sled a hundred miles in a day without ever questioning you. If they find you weak, they will tear your throats out as you sleep."

It was a simple message, and the Russian had learned from many centuries of experience. However, Saker and Sinter simply couldn't bring themselves to beat the dogs as he insisted they should. And now that they were reunited with them, they threw themselves into the mass of paws and fur. Sinter remembered to approach Yantar first.

Yantar means "Amber". He was named for the fact that one eye was iceberg blue like most Siberian huskies, but the other was a glorious golden amber colour, exactly like Sinter's own eyes. While this bizarre and beautiful coincidence cemented her affection and connection to Yantar, that was not why she approached him first. Yantar was the "lead" in the team. He was a dog of great intelligence and loyalty. A dog that could be counted upon to take the team safely across thin ice, or to find the best route up a steep and rocky hillside. On difficult terrain, Yantar would not even be harnessed, but would run on just ahead of his team, nose to the ground, senses on high alert, picking his way without the sled to hold him back. By showing Yantar affection first, Sinter was keeping to pack politics. If she'd gone to one of the lower-ranking dogs, Yantar would have had to wade in with flashing teeth and deal out some discipline.

Yantar was the key and had cost more than the whole of the rest of the ten-dog team put together, but he was worth every penny. Pups like him were rare, and the Russian had not wanted to part with him.

But for now no-one would ever guess his seniority in the team. Yantar was standing with both paws planted on Sinter's shoulders, licking her face, slobbering around her mouth as a wolf pup licks its mother's face to get her to regurgitate food. Sinter obviously couldn't do that, but she could hand out treats of stringy dried caribou meat, which the dogs snapped up as if they hadn't eaten in months!

For a moment the seriousness of their mission was forgotten, Sinter and Saker rolled in the snow with their canine friends, laughing at their frantic urge to play, and of course to run.

After half an hour, Saker's expression turned serious, and he looked up at the sky again. "This weather may not be changing as fast as I thought," he mused. "But it is going to change, and when it does it'll be brutal."

Sinter groaned. She knew what that meant. Digging a snow cave or making an igloo was a tortuous process. The last few nights they'd merely flattened out a spot under the boughs of a low-hanging conifer. They'd built a log wall to stave off the wind and to reflect the warmth of the fire back onto them, but that hadn't taken more than half an hour to put together. A good snow cave would take four hours.

First they found a snow ridge, where the snow had been blown over an edge to form a breaking wave shape called a cornice. They tested it to make sure it wouldn't collapse, but the snow was packed firm, and there were no obvious fractures. The dogs watched expectantly as they took shovels and started to carve into the white wall. After the first hour, the dogs lost interest and lay down in the snow again, occasionally snuffling round the spots where the caribou meat had been tossed, in the faint hope they might have missed a sliver. Saker and Sinter cut two parallel doorways, then joined them up, digging a flat ledge inside the cave where they could sleep. Wind would blow over the top of the cornice, and they would stay warm inside. The snow seemed dry, but melted with the warmth of their hands, soaking their gloves. They went through three pairs of gloves each and would have to dry them out later by the fire, or the trip would be over.

It grew dark before they were done. At this time of year, the endless dark of winter had passed, and though the sun never fully rose above the horizon, there was both day and a night. The sky would be light blue for five or six hours a day. The cubby looked like the inside of a fridge freezer in need of defrosting, lit a ghostly green with glowsticks jammed into the walls. They pulled in some caribou skins to function as a mattress and placed their sleeping bags, wrapped up in waterproof bivvi bags to keep them dry, on top. With their shelter complete, they built a fire in the lee of the cornice, and set to melting snow so the dogs could drink. The dogs danced on the outskirts of the flames as they flickered off the ice wall. They had fed and slept, and now were in the mood for play.

"The moon has a halo!" Sinter said. Saker looked up. The almost-full moon cast enough light to read a book by, but had a strange shimmering quality, and around it was a ring, a complete circular rainbow.

"It's a corona," he explained. "It's caused by moonlight shining through ice crystals way up high. It means there's a change of weather on the way. It's going to get chilly." As if to prove his point, a gust of wind swept past them.

The fire guttered then burst into life again. Sinter shivered. How could it possibly get any colder than this?

Saker was about to explain more, when an other-worldly noise cut him short. It was like a far-off siren, wavering as it travelled down a city street. Then the wind dropped, and the sound became pure.

"Wolves," Saker said. Sinter cocked her head. It was the first time she'd ever heard a wolf howl. As she listened, the primordial tone increased in richness as more wolves joined in. Something about it cut right through to her guts. It was the wildest, saddest, most bewitching sound she had ever heard.

"They're mourning," Saker said. "They're calling out to their leader. The brother who's never coming home."

Suddenly, Yantar sat back on his haunches, raised his muzzle to the moon and let loose a howl of his own. Sinter, who had been straining to hear, jumped in surprise. "*A dog is only a few meals away from being a wolf,*" she remembered.

Within seconds, the whole team had joined in. The wolves might have been howling in mourning, but the huskies were howling from something even deeper. From a memory several thousand years old, at the end of an ice age when half the planet looked like Siberia and their wolf ancestors ranged over the entire Northern hemisphere. Sinter didn't just hear it, she felt it. Right from her boots up to the back of her throat. It spiked a longing in her she couldn't even begin to understand. And then without warning, there was another howl by her shoulder. She turned in astonishment to see Saker, head back, eyes shut, howling as if it was the most natural thing in the world.

She couldn't believe how easy it was. The sound uttered from her mouth, but came from another place altogether. Sinter howled until the cold wind scorched her throat, howled away all the pain, howled to her dead mother, betrayer father, abandoned homeland. There in the glowing white lunar light, the humans and their dogs joined in a chorus older than time. Saker and Sinter howled themselves hoarse, the dogs settled into restless pacing and quarrelling, but the wolves in the distance continued.

3

The wind started to whip up at around three in the morning. Sinter really needed to go for a wee, but there was no way she would crawl out of her toasty sleeping bag and go into the deep freeze. Their cave was pretty much identical to the dens dug by female polar bears as places to hibernate and give birth to their cubs. While the temperature outside was around minus 30, inside their little snow cave it was just below freezing, which was pretty much perfect. Any warmer, and their breathing and body heat would have started to melt the ceiling, and they'd have been kept awake all night with drips plopping on their faces.

Sinter stared at the walls, lit by the meagre green wash from the glowsticks, and – not for the first time – wondered how on earth she'd ended up here. The last year had contained such surreal adventures that they barely seemed possible. First she'd been kidnapped from her father's house in India by the boy who now lay next to her. He was on the run, trailed by "the Clan", a society of boys trained to be thieves and assassins, a society that he had been a part of since birth. The chase had taken them high into the Himalayas where they had witnessed the awful things humans do to animals, in the illegal trade in tigers. Then they had parted company, and she had finally lived her dream of helping a doctor in the slums of Vietnam.

The Clan though had been determined to track down Saker – and by her association with him, her too – and they had to flee once more. They'd ended up in Borneo, inadvertently, becoming environmental activists and bringing down a senior politician who was destroying the rainforests that local hunter-gatherers and wildlife relied on. Now they had become their own Clan. They were well-financed and had behind them Minh, a computer-hacking genius who could cripple big companies from the comfort of his own sofa in Vietnam. All they needed was projects where they could really make a difference. The plight of the wolves and the Nenet peoples in Siberia had seemed perfect. It had been a wonderful idea when they were sweating in the humidity of the Borneo forests, but now, shivering in an environment where everything was new, Sinter kind of wished they'd looked into a few other options.

The wind outside howled like a thousand wolves. Sinter buried her face in the caribou skin rug, smelled its musty comfort, and closed her eyes again.

Saker shook her awake while it was still dark. "The snow's coming down heavily," he said. "We'd better dig out the sleds and dogs, or we'll never find them again."

It was an awful shock to the system to wriggle out of her snug cocoon, and feel the icy wind on her face, but Sinter knew they had to be thorough about their routines. A broken gas stove or spilled fuel would mean no food or drink. A dog not firmly tied to a stake at night could escape and eat through a week's provisions in an hour. Soaking gloves left to freeze could lead to losing fingers. Boots not dried and kept warm would lead to frostbitten toes. The slightest mistake could be fatal.

The snow had come in hard and drifted right over the top of their camp. The sleds only just showed, slight humps under powdery ivory blankets. Some of the dogs were slow to wake, leaving Sinter petrified that they had frozen to death, but eventually all were accounted for, and she began the long task of feeding then harnessing them to the sled.

Only when all the dogs had been cared for, did she think about the hunger in her own belly. She got the stove roaring, making sure that the snow cave was still ventilated so no gasses would build up and asphyxiate them. Meanwhile Saker remained outside in the wind and snow, setting a portable satellite dish about the size of a dustbin lid and trying to aim it towards a cloudless piece of sky. Sinter was just serving up mugs of hot chocolate and porridge when he came in with the laptop.

"We have a message from Minh," he said. "He's sent through a whole dossier on this company."

Minh was a unique young man who Sinter had first met in Vietnam. Although he had few social skills, they'd formed a bond, and his uncanny gift with computers was simply genius. Sinter and Saker's quest had appealed to his sense of a challenge, and his love for illegally hacking into places he shouldn't! They both knew that the hacker network he was building would achieve more in the modern world than they ever could. Cyber-terrorism had been bringing computer users and businesses to a standstill for decades, it was about time the hackers actually put their skills to positive use.

After his success helping them in Borneo, Minh had become rather notorious online, gaining many admiring hacker contacts around the world who would gladly support his projects, although Saker liked to grumble. "Typical, I bet he wouldn't be so popular if they ever actually met him in person!"

Saker opened the document, wincing as he burned his tongue on searing hot chocolate. He passed the laptop over to his friend. They'd had to choose their make carefully. The liquid crystal in most displays would simply have frozen on most models. And a metal-cased version would have frozen to their fingers!

"RAM-Corp," Sinter read. "Russian-American oil and gas corporation, working together since the Cold War. Wow!" She stopped dead, then re-read the last few sentences over and again to make sure she'd got it right.

"Wow, what?" Saker looked up from his cocoa.

"Well, if I've got this right, they made $39 billion last year."

"$39 billion? That must make them one of the biggest companies in the world! How come I haven't heard of them?"

"I guess they're not like Apple or Ford, they don't need to convince mugs like us to buy their stuff. From the sounds of things they're not the kind of company that cares what people think of them." She was scrolling through the document.

"They specialise in getting oil and gas out of countries that are at war, or extremely poor. Seems they make deals with corrupt politicians, and then pump all the fuel over the borders to places they can ship it round the world."

"That sounds like stealing!" Saker muttered.

"Yup," Sinter agreed. "But if you steal a car you go to prison. Steal the fuel to run a million cars and you get very, very rich."

"It all sounds a bit big for us," said Saker. "What does this have to do with our wolves?"

"That's where this guy comes in." Sinter swivelled the laptop around. On the screen was the face of what looked like a gunslinger in an old Western movie. He wore a ten-gallon Stetson hat, a string tie and a tan so deep it looked as if his skin had been soaked in creosote. "He's called Hep Rylander," she read.

"Hep Rylander?" Saker retorted. "Sounds like an actor in a bad action movie. Or an ointment for something itchy!"

Sinter didn't smile.

"Yeah, from what it says here, Hep was brought up in Minnesota. Went to Sunday school and everything, but that was where his good deeds ended. His family had all been into ranching, but in his twenties he moved to Texas and got into the oil business. He's now one of the richest men in the world, with like-minded influential friends in high places . . ."

"Figures," Saker huffed, and got stuck into his congealing porridge.

"Ah, here's something," Sinter moved down to a new page. "This growing up on a ranch in Minnesota thing. This seems to be where the wolves come in."

Saker was all ears.

"So in America, ranchers hate wolves."

Saker nodded, this wasn't news to him. Before settlers moved across America, wolves had been the most widespread mammal predator on earth. They had been systematically exterminated, hundreds of thousands turned into fur coats, victims of greed and unjustified hatred.

"Hep has been a key part in getting wolf hunts made legal again in a number of US states. He pulls strings and suddenly the laws swing against the wolves."

31

Sinter didn't have to look up; she knew Saker's expression would be one of utter disgust. She turned the laptop round to him again. It showed a photograph of a young boy with a rifle, kneeling over the corpse of a mighty wolf. Standing behind him, with a proud hand on his shoulder was the grinning perma-tanned face of Hep Rylander. "His twelve-year-old son. It was his birthday present to shoot a wolf," she explained.

The next few photos showed Hep himself standing with his foot on shot trophy specimens of grizzly bear, moose, and even in Africa with elephant and rhino. But most photos were of him and wolves. Dead wolves, their blood staining the snow.

"He's obsessed with hunting, and loathes wolves," Sinter said. "Every time he seals a big deal with someone he gives them a fur coat made from wolf skin as a present. It's his trademark. But there are so few wolves left in America now, that it's getting too difficult to find them."

"And let me guess," Saker cut in. "He's come to Russia to find a fresh stock of wolves."

"Those ranchers hate wolves so bad, it's just engrained. It's too tough out here for him to bother going out hunting himself. Instead he's offered a bounty to anyone who brings him in a quality wolf pelt. He won't rest until the whole species is annihilated."

Saker took from his pocket the wooden bullet that had also been there the last few weeks. Using it as their calling card had been Sinter's idea. The wood was fine tropical ironwood, a symbol of the treasures the wild world had to offer. Carving it into a bullet was supposed to provide a menacing omen to their target. A symbol of death. The hope was that after a few more missions like their success in Borneo, people would come to hear of the wooden bullet and know what it meant. Anyone who was doing bad things to animals or the environment would receive one, as a warning to change their ways.

But this was only the second bullet Saker had carved. Such things were still just a dream. This particular bullet had been polished to a fine sheen by the constant fidgeting of Saker's nervous fingers. At the base, where the firing cap would be on a real bullet, was the branded image of a Saker falcon's head.

"So do we have any idea when this Minnesota-born, Texas oilman who spends most of his time hob-nobbing with senators in Washington DC . . . is actually going to be in this part of Siberia?"

Sinter paused before responding. "Soon. He's due to tour the oil works in the next few days, and is also picking up a consignment of wolf skins. That could even have been his chopper we saw flying over us yesterday."

"OK," Saker was warming to the task. "So we use the storm as cover. We get as close as possible using the dogs, then head in at night. We cut through the fence, find his apartments, break in, and leave the bullet on the pillow next to him while he sleeps. He won't know what to do!" Saker's voice was rising in excitement so much that some of the dogs outside heard, and yipped and yelped, thinking they'd soon be leaping into action. "He'll be so scared he'll wet himself."

Sinter raised an eyebrow. She still hadn't been stoic enough to bare her bottom to the wind and her bladder was fit to burst! "Or he'll think someone's playing a joke on him. Or it'll slip down the back of the pillow and he won't even find it," she responded.

Saker frowned. Why wasn't she joining in? Finally their mission had found its target.

"What I don't get, is why we have to do this at all," she said. "Why don't we just get Minh to do his work, mess up his computers with worms and things? Steal his money from a distance rather than risking our lives with all this cloak and dagger rubbish. It's too risky and macho for me."

Saker faltered. He had to admit she had a point. But then he also felt he needed to face his enemy in the flesh. To smell their breath and sweat. And though he would never admit it, the "cloak and dagger rubbish" was what he had spent his whole life training for. The Clan had taken him as a baby, and devoted his every waking hour to becoming a silent assassin of the shadows, swift and ruthless like his namesake and totem the Saker falcon. If his new Clan had no place for such skills, Saker himself was redundant.

"We have to give them a warning," he said. "A chance to change and become a force for good rather than greed.

They're not going to take that seriously if it comes in an email. And besides, if we can make this work a few times, then all we'll have to do is send the bullet. The bad guys will know what it means straightaway."

He took out the piece of parchment on which a few simple words were inscribed:

Continue to take from the planet what is most valuable, and we will take what is most valuable from you. Poison our world and we will poison yours. Continue to take lives, and yours too will be taken.

The Ghosts of the Forest

"An eye for an eye, and a tooth for a tooth," Saker quoted.

Sinter sighed. "I'll harness the dogs."

4

Something wasn't right. Normally the dogs battled to be first into the harnesses, desperate to get to work and run the sled. It usually took all Sinter's strength to restrain them, and their natural enthusiasm would result in squabbles between them. This morning though they were shying away, barking with little high-pitched yips. Even Yantar didn't want to put his harness on.

"What is it, boy?" she said. "Don't want to work today?"

But it wasn't the harness that was spooking him. He was looking off into the snow over her shoulder. Suddenly he gave a sharp bark, and lifted his upper lip in a snarl. Sinter jumped. She had never seen him bare his teeth before. Her first thought was to scold him, but she knew his senses were much keener than her own. What was it he could smell or see?

And then she smelled it herself. The dry air changed

direction for a second and carried a damp odour their way. The smell of a big animal.

She turned just in time; the huge white paw came out of nowhere. Great curved claws sliced centimetres away from her face, she felt the draft as it whistled past her cheeks. Yantar leapt forward, white fangs snapping together in fury, but his harness held him back. The next swipe from the near invisible giant cuffed the dog with sickening force, silencing him and throwing his body to the ground, before knocking Sinter flat on her back. The huge white creature drew itself up to its full height, standing taller than two men, and let out a roar that would've thawed the frozen dead. Sinter lay helpless looking at her first ever polar bear. It was the one animal in this white world she knew to fear. Not many animals on earth will hunt and eat a human. A big crocodile perhaps, but if you stay out of their rivers you're safe. Here though, the polar bear roamed where it wished. Clever, quick, cunning and utterly terrifying.

She lay paralysed, waiting for the second when the enormous paws would come down to crush her skull . . . And then the great bear's gaze left hers. Something had distracted it. Around them the snow was alive with furious, screaming spirits. Saker had loosed the dogs and, incensed, they were leaping towards their ancient enemy, snapping at his heels, then leaping back again before he could land a blow.

Saker sprinted with the dogs, standing as tall as could make himself, yelling and swinging his arms, trying to distract the bear make it attack him rather than his friend. Sinter, still dazed, watched as if in a dream. She saw heavy snowflakes twirling in the air like fairy sprites, saw the wind ruffle the thick hairs at the scruff of Yantar's lifeless neck, noticed that the boy had not put his down jacket on, and would surely be cold. The bear swinging out at her dogs looked like King Kong on top of the Empire State building, throwing punches at passing planes.

"Sinter! Sinter, the bear spray!"

She shook her head, clearing the fuzziness. Of course! The canister of bear spray she kept clipped to her belt. As she reached for it, the bear came crashing down, its paw the size of a dinner plate aimed straight at her face. She rolled at the last second, snatching the spray can in one motion, flipping off the cap, and unloading the spray in the bear's direction.

Bear spray is very much like the pepper spray that riot police use on unruly crowds. It's made of highly concentrated chilli peppers, so hot that they actually burn exposed skin. If it gets into the eyes and sensitive nose however, the pain is unbearable. These sprays work well on people, but on bears they are like a missile fired from a tank. The predator reeled, clawing at its nose in confusion and agony. He stumbled a few paces and sneezed, then turned back to his tormentors, and let loose a roar so horrific that Sinter had to clap her hands over her ears and press her face into the snow. Even the dogs leapt back yelping.

"Hit him again!" Saker yelled. Sinter came up to her knees, took careful aim, and unloaded the rest of the stream into the bear's face. This time the roar was one not of rage but extreme pain. Eyes streaming, nose on fire, the huge white hunter staggered, temporarily blind. All of a sudden he became the hunted, and he didn't like it a bit. He looked back one last time, blinking furiously through the tears, then took off at a gallop, lurching over the snow, stumbling into drifts he would normally have spotted with ease. The dogs took up the chase, something in their brains telling them to finish off their wounded enemy.

"Stop!" Saker yelled to the dogs. "Come back!" But their blood was up, and the sport was too good, the blood rushing in their ears drowned out his commands.

For now, that would have to wait. Saker dropped into the snow alongside Sinter, grabbing her shoulder.

"Are you hurt?"

"Don't worry about me," she said, "Yantar took the force of it. He jumped right in front of the bear. If he hadn't, I'd be . . ." She didn't finish her sentence. She didn't need to.

Saker knelt by Yantar. His eyes were shut and there were four ugly gashes from the bear's claws across his shoulder.

"Let's get him in the snow cave," he said, picking the dog up gently, cradling him like a baby.

Inside, Sinter took stock of the situation. She'd insisted on bringing a superbly stacked medical kit, but was only used to treating human beings.

"How different can it be?" Saker said. "He's just another mammal after all."

Sinter was about to snap at him for being so stupid, but didn't want to waste her breath. Instead, she took out her stethoscope, and started probing Yantar's chest. Where was a dog's heart anyway? And then she heard it, a faint double thump, and his heartbeat! It sounded exactly like a human's. Saker hadn't been so stupid after all.

As she set to work stitching his wounds, Saker got another fire going, and started boiling hot water. When he returned to the snow cave, it was with warming hot soup.

"Are the dogs back?" Sinter asked him.

"Not yet, but they'll come back soon enough."

"Will they kill it?" She asked, half with concern, half with hope.

Saker snorted. "Not likely. The polar bear is the biggest predator on earth – well, on average anyway – the occasional Kodiak grizzly gets bigger. The dogs will wise up and lose their nerve soon enough. As soon as their adrenaline wears off they'll be back here with their tails between their legs."

"And what about the bear?" Sinter asked. "Will he be back?"

This silenced Saker for a minute or so. "That I don't

know. It just depends how hungry he is. That's what makes them so dangerous. There's so little food out here that they need to take advantage of anything warm-blooded they can get their teeth into."

"You don't think the pepper spray will have put him off?" she said.

"For a while, but when it wears off, the next time he smells us he may come back to try and finish us off."

"But we should be miles away by then," Sinter reasoned.

"It won't be far enough," Saker replied seriously. "Polar bears have the best sense of smell of any animal. They've been seen walking forty miles in a straight line towards a dead seal. The only possible explanation is that they've smelled it. *From forty miles away!*"

"I guess that's why the spray works so well," Sinter said.

"Exactly," Saker said. "With a nose that sensitive the pain must be incredible. Did you see how quickly he changed his mind about eating you?"

Sinter was distracted from answering by a thin whine. "Yantar!" she exclaimed. The dog had woken up, wrapped in a caribou hide blanket. They could have kissed him. He clearly wasn't fit to stand, so they decided to keep him in the snow cave with them that night. Their mission would have to wait another day.

Hep Rylander was not a happy man. He'd spent most of his life under the big blue skies of Texas, where even in winter the sun never seemed to stop shining. And here he was, standing on a soggy carpet, with snow in his moustache.

"This better be making me a sack-load of cash." he cursed as he spat into the snow.

"D'yu think I enjoy dragging my sorry ass out here to this hellhole?" He berated his foreman. "You should know how to do your jobs. But I always have to be coming out here to the end of the darn world, checking up on you, or you'd be shipping my oil out to Tinkywinky-Stan or wherever it is you all come from."

Sergei, the foreman, briefly pondered telling Hep that no American owned their oil, and that everyone would be a lot happier if he'd just stay in Texas.

"I come from Moscow, Mr Hep, sir. It is a modern city;

I don't like the cold any more than you do. And we would not cheat you. As you can see with your own eyes, everything here is as it should be."

"That's bull and you know it." Hep was angry now. "My pipeline should have been finished two months ago. D'yu have any idea how much money it's cost me waiting for y'all to catch up?"

Sergei didn't know, but had a feeling Hep was about to tell him.

"More than you'd earn in a thousand lifetimes, Vladimir!"

Sergei didn't know if Hep was getting his name wrong on purpose just to be rude, or if he just didn't care what any of his minions were called.

"Mr Hep, sir, the environmental report has to be completed before we can build across the Yamal. There are people living here, and wildlife, and . . ." He realised he had made a mistake and stopped. Hep Rylander's face had turned beetroot beneath his tan.

"Environmental report?" he bellowed. "I can tell you what you can do with that. Print it out on nice soft paper, and put it in the men's room! You say those two words to me again, son, and I'll have them engraved on your stinking tombstone. There's nothing out there, boy. Nothing but snow, and maybe the odd Eskimos who ain't even got TV yet."

Sergei winced. Eskimos came from the other side of the Arctic, and even there the term was considered an insult. Again, he decided to be diplomatic and let it slide.

"And where are my wolf skins?" Hep demanded. "That's the only reason I come out here at all. I have meetings with a whole bunch of business partners from the Middle East, and they're expecting fur coats. If it weren't for them I coulda sent my son out here. He's only twelve, but he'd make a better job of it than y'all."

Sergei grimaced. "Please Mr Hep, sir, we have professional hunters out as we speak. I'm sure they have some results by now."

"They better had. Get my skins, and get my pipeline back on schedule, or I'll personally see to it that you spend the rest of your pitiful life picking icicles out of your butt."

Hep turned on his expensive leather boot heel, and stormed inside. Sergei had to admit, he had a creative way with language.

Hep tapped a four-digit code into the entry unit at the door to his suite. It swung open and he stepped inside. Walking through the main lounge area, he passed a polar bear, stuffed and mounted standing on its hind legs. There was also a taxidermy wolf, its lips drawn back into a snarl, and a pair of snowy owls. Even in death and stuffed with old rags they looked exquisite. He went into the kitchen, swung open the fridge door and cracked open a beer.

"Idiots," he cursed under his breath.

"I'm not sure they'd like being called that," a voice said.

Hep's beer smashed to the granite floor, spraying all over his hand-stitched leather boots.

"What the hell!" He looked up, to see a figure sitting casually at his table. "Who in Sam Hill are you? And how did you get in here?" The figure turned on the table lamp, illuminating his features. It was a boy! He was in his mid-teens and, with his dark, close-cropped hair and penetrating gaze, he was imposing. His eyes burned with an intensity that would have been unsettling. If Hep had been the kind of man to be unsettled.

"You have about twenty seconds to start talking, boy, then I'm going to come over there, put you over my damn knee, and spank your bottom blue!"

The figure remained impassive. "Mr Rylander, we have been watching you for some time now. Your actions here in the Yamal, and elsewhere have been remarkably . . . *ruthless*." The last word was carefully chosen. Every instinct in Rylander's being was telling him to storm over and give the kid a good hiding, but there was something about him, something about his unflappable calm, something about the way he held himself. How could the kid be so confident?

"You don't even know the meanin' of ruthless, boy. Now start talking."

The boy shifted in his chair, as if he was in a car seat and preparing himself for a long journey. "Some years ago, you had a problem with The Feldstrom Corporation, they were outbidding you for part of the East Timor oilfield." Hep stiffened. The boy had his attention.

"You paid our organisation to make the problem go away."

Hep stuttered, then snapped back. "That was you? Yeah I remember, you're a bunch of con artists! I paid a small fortune, then old man Feldstrom went and died of a heart attack. You didn't do squat, and I got the contract anyway. The way I figure it, you all owe me a couple of million, plus interest!"

He was about to grab the phone and call security, when he realised the boy had produced a tiny glass vial, and was rolling it nonchalantly between his fingers. "What you got there, boy?"

"This? This is Tetradotoxin. It's one of the strongest natural poisons. You get it from the bite of the blue-ringed octopus; it's no bigger than a golf ball, but has a bite that can kill. It's also found in the organs of puffer fish. Believe it or not, some Japanese eat the puffer fish with just enough poison in it to set their lips tingling . . . they call it the kiss of death."

Hep's eyes widened.

"In larger doses though, it is totally lethal. It paralyses you, giving the exact symptoms of a heart attack. Easy to administer if you know how, leaves no trace, the perfect assassin's tool." The boy eased himself back into his chair. "I mean, I could easily have put some in any one of the bottles of beer in your fridge. Really, it's child's play." He returned the vial to his pocket. Hep sat down. The colour had drained from his face.

"So that's what you're here for? To kill me?" He was suddenly aware that his mouth was parched. He could do with one of those beers. Or then again that might be a very bad idea. "Whatever they're paying you boy, I'll double it, right now." The boy held up his hand and cut Hep short. Suddenly he was in complete control.

"If I'd been here for that, you would never have seen my face or heard my voice. No, I'm here to ask a favour."

"A favour?" Hep nearly choked. "What is this, blackmail?" and then he remembered himself. "What kind of favour?"

The boy leaned forward. Hep saw for the first time that his eyes were almost golden, they reminded him of something familiar, something animalistic he couldn't quite place.

"Some time in the next few days you are going to get an uninvited visitor," the boy said. "He will come in the night, and he will mean you harm. We've been following his communications for weeks now and we know he's coming here for you."

"But this place is like Fort Knox," Hep interrupted. "He'll never get anywhere near me!" And then he looked at the boy sitting at his table, and realised how ridiculous his statement was.

"He is very well-trained. The security here will not be sufficient. My request is simple. Let me and my colleague stay here, and be waiting for him when he comes. We will take care of him. That is all."

"Sooo, you want to protect me?" Hep was incredulous. "What's it going to cost?"

The boy shook his head. "Nothing."

"You want to protect me, and you don't want any money? What is this?"

"Just make sure you remember us Mr Rylander. Some day we may well call on you, but it won't be for money."

"I might have known there'd be a catch." He thought for a few seconds. "Well then sure. Sure, I guess. But who is this we? And who the hell are you?"

"Who I represent is not important," the boy said, standing to leave the room. "And you can call me Wolf."

6

It had been the sleepless night to end all sleepless nights. Saker and Sinter had decided to take it in turns to stand guard watching for the bear. The storm was in full swing now, and the wind gusted through camp like a thousand spirit knives, cutting into their flesh. The chill was much easier to ignore if they were moving, but sitting keeping watch made them feel as if their blood would freeze. There was no relief in the cave either; Yantar was hurting and restless. Sinter hadn't wanted to give him any pain-relief drugs, as she didn't know how they might affect a dog, so he rolled and whined throughout the night.

As the wind whistled past the entrance, it turned the snow-cave into a huge wind instrument, making sounds that played tricks on their ears. One second it would echo as if to the roar of a polar bear nearby, the next it would be a police car siren, before transforming into the scream of a teething baby. Sinter wrapped the caribou hide around her head, but just as she was drifting off she heard the baying of the dogs coming back to them. She sat up in alarm, instantly wide awake, then realised it was a cruel trick of the storm. Settling down again, she heard someone calling her name; "Sinter, Sinter, Sinter." Again, the second she sat up, the whispers faded away.

Shortly after dusk, the dogs really did come back. Sinter was on watch, and took their barks for more cruel trickery, but then two canine shapes appeared out of the blizzard, tails between their legs, expecting to be beaten for their impetuousness. It was the two wheel dogs. They're the dogs always hitched at the back of the team, closest to the sled, and need to be the most cautious, steady and calm in temperament, so as not to be constantly freaked out by the sled being right on top of them. Their personalities had clearly led to them seeing sense first, giving up the chase and returning to their masters.

One by one the other dogs trailed into camp, tired, hungry, but not injured. Only one dog failed to return. Knoyok (which means "Patch") was a team dog, one of those who provide muscle in the centre. He had always been eager and enthusiastic, as well as totally tireless, but had not been the brightest, and often got himself tangled in his tethers. It seemed obvious that he would be the one who would have been the most reckless in his pursuit of the polar bear. Saker and Sinter waited hours after all the others had returned, before finally accepting Patch was not coming back.

"I'm just surprised only one dog got killed really," Saker said. "Chasing an angry polar bear, they could all have had a nasty end."

"But what if he's only injured?" Sinter asked. "What if he's lying out there in the cold in pain?"

"Then he is already covered by snow. His tracks are covered, and he won't be able to generate enough body heat. If he isn't dead now, he soon will be."

"But surely we should look?" Sinter pleaded. "The team is two dogs down now."

"And if we go out there in this weather to search, we will probably lose another dog, and possibly one of us too." Saker was firm. "There are different rules out here, you have to abide by them."

Sinter didn't like it, but she knew he was right. After a few forlorn calls of "Patch, Patch," which were instantly carried away by the wind, they packed their gear, leaving their food, cooking stoves, fuel and sleeping bags in the snow cave. Sinter sat on top of the sled, with Yantar laid across her lap. Saker took the standing position at the back to steer the team. The brake was a step at the back that he could press into the snow to create drag, and if the sled needed to be kept stationary, there was an anchor that could be stamped into the snow.

With the dogs harnessed, but the sled anchored, it was absolute bedlam. They barked, snarled and snapped at each other's flanks, the anticipation of running brewing inside them, and boiling over in aggression. Saker rocked the sled from side to side to break the runners free from the ice, then pulled out the anchor and shouted "Mush!"

Instantly the dogs transformed. They strained forward, then as soon as the sled gained some momentum fell into their stride. From then on there was total silence, the dogs overwhelmed by the joy of running. Sinter looked at her team – utterly in their element – and wondered how on earth anyone could keep a husky as a pet. Particularly in a cramped apartment in a city. These dogs had been bred for thousands of years to run all day long; they'd comfortably go a hundred miles a day!

Usually they'd run the team for an hour, then stop for a rest. The dogs would look exhausted, panting great clouds of steam, tongues lolling out of their mouths, chests heaving. Then within a minute or two, their breathing would be back to normal. Leave it any longer, and they'd be crying out, demanding more! These were dogs of the white wilds, only a step away from their wolf cousins.

Saker too seemed to have been infected by the ecstasy of the chase. The wind was slicing their faces, Sinter's dark Indian skin had turned pale and blotchy. She had her hood pulled tight around her, trying not to expose anything to the elements. Occasionally she'd plunge her nose into Yantar's warm fur until she could barely breathe. Saker however seemed oblivious to the cold. His hood was thrown back, eyebrows and nostrils iced over so he looked like Jack Frost!

Yantar whined a little in Sinter's lap. Perhaps he was dreaming. Not for the first time, she wondered what she had got herself into. Somewhere out there in the storm was an unpredictable confrontation. Who knows what they would find? Saker though was alive with new purpose, like a soldier who'd been given his orders. Things were so much simpler for him Sinter mused; he was like the dogs – he ran, he ate, he slept, he ran again. Any more than that and he'd get confused or irritable! He didn't worry about things like why they were on this mission, like whether they lived or died. Sometimes he seemed just like a living breathing robot. She envied the black and white simplicity of his world.

They ran the dogs for three hours, following the compass because they couldn't see more than a few metres ahead. While the dogs got their breath back, Sinter threw them chunks of frozen seal blubber, and Saker studied the map.

"We're getting close," he said, and pointing into the gloom. "The pipeline is only a few hundred metres that way, it'd be a piece of cake to take a lump of plastic explosive and blow the thing sky high."

"And flood a pristine environment with oil?" Sinter retorted. "In order to stop them pumping it out for a week? That's pretty thoughtless even for you!"

"Just an idea." Saker said sulkily. It was clear he really hadn't thought it through!

"So what do we do now?" Sinter asked.

Saker frowned. "I reckon we move another mile or so,

then go in on foot at night. We need to leave the dogs here 'cos they'll be too noisy."

"And then what? Won't the compound be guarded?"

"Of course," Saker replied. "But I'd be amazed if it's tight security. They're a thousand miles from the nearest town, no environmentalists could get out here and hassle them. Trust me, after what we've done before, this will be easy!"

Sinter smiled. On their last mission in Borneo, they had broken into an executive's office suite, hacked his computer, and emptied his bank accounts. That was how they were so well-funded now. Saker was right, by comparison, this would be a walk in the park.

They went the last mile at a pace the dogs couldn't understand. Why were their masters not allowing them to run? Instead they crept over the snow at no more than walking speed. The runners sank further into the snow, making the sled harder to drag. Finally, they reached an escarpment, an extended ridge-line that provided cover for the sled and dogs, not to mention some respite from the endless gales. As darkness approached, the dogs dug alcoves in the snow, walked around and around, nose to tail, as their wolf cousins still do to flatten out their bed, before lying down for the night.

Saker and Sinter's day though was just beginning. Sinter took care to dress Yantar's wound, and wrap the injured animal on their sled in caribou skins. To her relief, Yantar lapped some warmed milk from her flask, then ate a few small scraps of seal blubber. He still whined a little, but licked his lips and then Sinter's fingers. The dog was strong and had great spirit.

"He'll recover fine in a few days," Sinter told Saker. "If he's given the right care. If we can keep him warm and feed him like a baby."

"Well, that's great!" Saker responded.

"IF," Sinter reiterated. "If we give him the right care. On the other hand, if we go off on some crazy mission, and leave him to freeze . . ." She didn't need to finish.

"This is what we've come all this way for, Sinter," Saker said. "If you've decided to bottle out, then fine. But we've travelled thousands of miles to get here, we have a plan, and I'm going to carry it out, with or without you."

"I'm not bottling out," she protested indignantly. "I just think we could wait a few days, let him get strong."

"This is our chance," Saker said. "The storm gives us extra cover, it'll make it easier for us to get in, and harder for them to chase us afterwards. The storm will blow over in a day or two, by which time we could already be back in town, sipping hot tea and getting Yantar some proper medical help."

Sinter was about to launch into the argument, but stopped herself. He did have a point. They'd come a long way for this, and if she was honest with herself, she was scared. Maybe that was the real reason she was trying to delay their nocturnal mission. Perhaps she should take Saker's example, stop thinking so much and just do it.

"We go tonight, place the bullet, plus any sabotage we can get away with." He looked at her. "Without flooding the Yamal with oil . . . and then we're gone. We'll be no more than a whisper. They'll never even know we were there, the only thing we leave behind is fear."

Sinter nodded. They would go.

The pair streamlined their kit, taking only essentials from the sled, which they packed into small rucksacks. They covered their heavy down jackets with white smocks, which camouflaged them perfectly. Sinter knew she'd warm up as soon as they got moving. After strapping on their snowshoes, they covered the sled with a groundsheet.

"The snow will soon settle on it," Saker said, taking GPS co-ordinates from the area. "No-one's going to find it except us."

Despite having broad snowshoes to keep them from sinking too far into the softer snow, it was a battle to trudge along the length of the ridge, often plunging up to their knees with every step. It was even worse, because they needed to keep their torches off and had to allow their eyes to get accustomed to the faint natural light. Time and again, they would stumble into drifts, and have to battle their way out of the deepest bits, lungs scorched with the effort and icy air.

It was two in the morning when the first orange glow of the compound lights broke through the swirling hurricane of the blizzard. The howling winds carried away any sounds from the plant's machinery and there was a diseased quality to the distorted yellowy haloes round every lamp. Gradually, as they got closer they could make out the rusting grey and black cooling towers, topped with flame and billowing black smoke. The place looked like a moon-base on some alien planet.

Saker and Sinter huddled behind a mound that was probably a shrub, covered in layers of snow. Saker took a rifle night-sight out of his backpack, and cast it over the compound. The infra-red sight magnified the sparse light there was and gave the vista a strange green tint. He studied every square metre with care.

"OK, it's just what we thought," he shouted in Sinter's ear. He felt as though he should have been whispering, but the wind made that impossible. "The storm's kept all the guards inside in the warm. There's no-one there at all. I reckon that building there, behind the helicopter, must be where Rylander's quarters are. It has windows for natural light, and looks like the newest bit of the place. The lights are off though, so if he's in, he's asleep."

"So what's our next move?" shivered Sinter through gritted teeth.

"We go in under the wire by the main generator," Saker answered. "Cut the power to the main lights, and head over in darkness. I should be able to bypass the keypad by the door, then we get inside and find our way to Rylander's rooms."

Sinter gave him a gloved thumbs up.

They unbuckled their snowshoes, stashing them under

the shrub. Saker counted three, then they dashed as fast as they could across the snow to the fence. They were relieved to see it was not electrified, and Saker's bolt cutters were through it in a few decisive clips. He cut a semi-circular hole, and bent the wire back to give them enough room to wriggle through. Once they were both inside, they crawled over the chilly white carpet to the concrete outbuilding that housed the electricity generators. There was a broad lever that held the door shut. It wasn't locked. The door swung open and they stepped inside. For the first time in days they were suddenly free from the wind. It was pitch black inside the bunker, and after the ceaseless wind battering their senses, it seemed deathly silent. Saker switched on his torch, and they swept the walls, finally finding a series of orange levers, marked with the international lightning flash symbol that stands for power.

"Here goes nothing," Saker said, and pulled all the levers. There was a sighing noise as the plant powered down. Then silence. Stepping back out into the wind, they saw their plan had worked. All the lights had extinguished, the cooling towers, silos and warehouses stood in eerie darkness.

It was several hundred metres of open space to get to the door. The pair covered it as fast as they could, and arrived panting, breath smoking in the blackness. The keypad was the bit Saker had been really worried about. These things could be a nightmare to circumvent. He took from his backpack the black wallet that contained his expensive new security bypassing kit, but to his astonishment, before he could even touch the keypad, the door hissed, and popped open. They looked at each other in amazed silence. What a stroke of luck! Shutting down the power must have cut out more than just the lights. This place really wasn't at all worried about security!

They stepped inside, and found themselves in a corridor, leading to several stairwells, with thick concrete walls, metal stairs and handrails. The place was like a nuclear bunker. They tiptoed up the first flight of stairs, careful not to clang on the steel. They needn't have bothered. It was silent as a tomb. Nobody moving, not a sound.

Eventually Sinter hissed, "Saker. What's going on? Where is everybody? This is too easy!"

He knew exactly what she meant. People should be dashing around trying to put the power back on again. No matter how remote they were, this was a multi-billion dollar processing plant, there had to be security active every hour of day and night. Why was it all so quiet?

"Maybe they just had a heavy night on the vodka," he answered. "I don't know." But he didn't believe his own words. "Let's just do this thing and get out of here, before they all wake up."

They chose a corridor, and moved cautiously down it, but as their backs turned a closed circuit camera mounted high on the wall, blinked on a red light. With a faint mechanical whirring, it swivelled to follow Saker and Sinter's progress.

7

Wolf had watched every single move Saker and Sinter had made once they'd entered the compound on a bank of cameras in the command centre above Rylander's apartment. Saker and Sinter would have been shocked to see how wrong they were about the level of security, which was actually state-of-the-art. They had been picked up by thermal imaging cameras as they cut through the outer fence. The cameras saw not light, but heat. Against the black of the cold background, their bodies had glowed orange and yellow, especially their faces, where bare hot skin was exposed. They had not really shut down the power either. Wolf had ordered the outside lighting to be switched off just as Saker had flipped the lever.

By Wolf's side stood Snowy Owl, a Clan boy whose penetrating eyes took in everything around him. He watched Wolf as he gazed into the cameras, noticed him leaning forward with anticipation as Saker and Sinter sprinted across the snow. As Saker stared in amazement at the safety door popping open in front of them, Wolf looked through the close-up camera into the face of his adversary. Snowy Owl noted Wolf biting his lip, his fists clenching and unclenching. It was all Wolf could do not to fly off the leash and rage down the corridors after his quarry.

"Patience," said Snowy Owl calmly. "Just let them get into Rylander's apartment. We'll lock them inside, then pump in gas, and go in once they're out cold. That way there's no danger to any of us."

"Are you saying I can't take them?" Wolf's response was so fiery that Snowy Owl actually stepped back. "Are you saying they're too much for me to handle?"

"No, no!" Snowy Owl protested. "I just . . . well, they have escaped before. It's best to be safe."

"Forget safe," Wolf was rabid with hatred now. "They're not going anywhere. There's a thousand miles of ice out there, they can't run this time. I'm going to crush them like cockroaches."

"But the Prophet said to bring them in alive!"

"I know what the Prophet said," snapped Wolf. "We've made that mistake before. This time, they're going back in a body bag."

Snowy Owl cocked his head, uncertain, showing his concern. Wolf actually snapped his teeth. The quieter boy raised his hands in the universal gesture of surrender.

Wolf switched his attention back to the cameras. Saker and Sinter were taking the bait, like tigerfish going after a silver spinner, lured onto an irresistible hook.

However, he didn't want to make it too easy. Sooner or later they would realise that something was up. He looked back at the screens. So far the intruders hadn't seen a living soul. The route was so obvious it almost seemed they were following a bunch of signposts saying; "this way to Hep Rylander's place"! Wolf watched as after the clanging metal floors they came to a corridor lined with thick carpet, the walls decorated with artwork and sculptures. It didn't fit in with the gloomy grey industrial feel of the rest of the plant. They knew they were close. Wolf zoomed in on one of the thermal cameras. Saker was turning something in his pocket over and over in his fingers. Something dark, cool, inanimate. Wolf frowned. What could that be?

Finally the corridor turned a corner, and before them was the door that must surely lead to their goal. There was another keypad. As they moved in closer, Wolf willed them on, step by step, tiptoeing towards the trap.

"Go on . . . go on," he breathed, grasping the edges of the screen till his knuckles turned white. Suddenly, he froze, as Sinter turned and looked up right into the camera. Her gaze was so intense that it felt as if she was looking directly at him, face to face. Instinctively Wolf stepped back, but then stopped himself; that was ridiculous, she couldn't see back through the cameras. Nevertheless, she was studying the camera intently. And now she was calling Saker over.

"What are they saying?" Wolf asked anxiously. "Can I get some sound on this feed?"

A technician typed a few lines into a keyboard, and pressed a button, there was a crackle, feedback, then Saker's voice came through over a tinny loudspeaker.

"It's active," they heard Saker say. "Look, you can see the lens focusing."

"Someone's watching us," Sinter said.

"So why hasn't anyone come?" It was Saker's voice now, his face distorted and fat-looking as he stared into the camera lens.

"Because it's a trap!" Sinter barked. There was a beat while Saker's mind processed this information.

"RUN!" he yelled, and the group in the command centre saw Saker make a motion that must have been tearing the wires out of the back of the camera, for the screen instantly turned black.

"NO!" Wolf smashed his fist on the desk, then sprinted for the door. Snowy Owl took his coat from the back of his chair, and walked after him, pausing only to pick up a pistol, and a vial of clear liquid.

The second they had ripped the cables from the camera, the power burst back on, the corridors lit up and a deafening klaxon started to sound. The pair hurdled down the stairs as if they were on a helter-skelter, taking entire flights at a time as they clattered over the metal.

"Stupid, stupid STUPID!" Saker cursed as he flew. He should have known, it had all been way too easy. He had been lured like a beast to a baited trap. As they rounded a corner, they came face to face with two guards running towards them, hefty machine guns in their hands. They were too slow for Saker. He jumped feet first and slid along the floor, then at the last second thrust one foot up into one guard's groin, before sweeping both his legs away. It looked almost as if he was break-dancing, but was deceptively effective. The guard hit the ground like a lassoed bison, the air driven from his lungs on impact. Saker came straight up into a crouching position, and struck at the weapon in the other guard's hands, as he struggled to bring his gun round to aim at his target. Saker wrenched it towards himself, taking the guard off-balance, before propelling it backwards into the guard's midriff. As he exhaled, Saker drove the butt of the gun up into his chin. The second adversary dropped with the same finality as the first.

Sinter hadn't even broken stride, she had reached the end of the corridor and the door that led outside. Only this time it was not going to just spring open and invite them through. This time it was locked with all the technology a billion dollar institution could muster. Saker stared at the keypad in dismay. Nine numbers on the keypad, a four-digit code, and no time to try to hack it.

"Fingerprints!" Sinter exclaimed, and pointed.

Alongside the keypad, she'd spotted a fingerprint recognition screen; a scan of unique fingerprints would bypass the need for a code.

"How does that help?" Saker asked.

"The guards!" Saker instantly understood. They turned as one, and sprinted back down the corridor. One of the two guards was still unconscious on the floor. The other was dazed, trying to help himself up using the wall for support. Saker hit him with a single blow knocking him back down. Quickly they sized up the two burly Russians, chose the least heavy, and started to drag him, the shiny metal floor for once helping them.

As they came to the corner, the clanging sound of multiple military boots thundered towards them, and four more guards came into view, brandishing weapons. Saker flinched, waiting for the fatal bullets to tear him to shreds, and yelled as the report flashed out, a volley of automatic machine-gun fire that felt as if it would split the world apart. But then he realised it wasn't coming from the guards at all. Sinter had taken the machine gun from their unconscious guard, pointed it in roughly the right direction and pulled the trigger. An entire magazine of bullets emptied throughout the corridor, ricocheting down the hall, bouncing off the metal floor and walls.

Sinter was thrown bodily backwards by the recoil, as the gun unleashed its lethal load. Bullets whizzed and zipped, and the guards fell back in disarray. It gave Saker just enough time to drag the unconscious body a few metres more towards the keypad, stretch out the guard's arm, and place his thumb onto the screen. There was a second of silence. Saker heard the renewed clanging and echoing shouts as the guards regrouped, he heard the drip as a single drop of sweat beaded on his nose and fell to the cold steel floor. He saw fear crystallise in Sinter's amber eyes as she looked at the screen, and then, in desperation at him. In slow motion he heard the sigh and hiss as the door slid open, like a door inside the Starship Enterprise. Saker took the gun from Sinter's hands, and smashed the fingerprint screen to smithereens. The last thing he heard was the swish of the door shutting, as he ran after her out into the snow.

Wolf raced towards the sounds of the shots and zipping, bouncing bullets, screaming with blood lust and frustration. "NO! He's mine! No-one kills him but me!" He leapt over the prostrate form of the unconscious guard and up to the door. Three Russian guards were falling over each other in their attempts to bypass the lock, Wolf could see instantly it was in vain. The runaways had escaped into the storm, and he couldn't follow.

Snowy Owl, however, had taken a different path. His totem animal is uncommonly canny, wily. Unlike a wild dog that takes its prey head on, chasing it to exhaustion in an overt and upfront attack, such birds of prey use night, silence and surprise as weapons, and they don't waste their energy. A small rodent such as a lemming will be looking the other way grooming its whiskers, when mighty talons snatch it from the snow. Snowy Owl lived up to his name. He strode purposefully, but without unnecessary speed, in the opposite direction to Wolf. As he walked, he pulled his thick jacket on, then took a small metal syringe, about the size and shape of his thumb from the inside pocket. He pushed the needle into the glass vial he had just picked up, and filled it with fluid. Then, still walking, he slotted the syringe into the chamber of the pistol.

He cocked the gun with the syringe in place ready to be fired, then pushed open a heavy metal door that led onto a balcony two storeys up. Instantly, he was blasted by raging wind, which took the breath from his lungs. He'd been inside all day and night, and was unprepared for the ferocity of the cold. Bracing himself, he looked down onto the courtyard beneath, and the two figures sprinting as fast as they could through the thick slush.

Snowy Owl raised the pistol to his eyeline. Though they both wore the same white smocks, one was taller, and had an athletic gait. It was undoubtedly Saker. Snowy Owl closed his eyes and relaxed, he forced his breathing to still, and the sights of the pistol steadied, the silhouette of the boy tight between them. He squeezed the trigger.

There was a spark from the perimeter fence. Snowy cursed. The wind was stronger than he'd anticipated and had blown his bullet off trajectory. Calmly he took another syringe dart from his pocket, filled it from the vial as if he had hours to spare. "Better get it right this time." As he slotted the syringe into the gun, he saw that Saker had already dropped to his belly to slide through the hole in the fence, and was no longer a clear target. Snowy changed his target to the girl, who was still running. Breathing out long and slow, he squeezed the trigger.

8

As Saker scrabbled under the wire, the snow funnelled under his jacket and into his thermal layers. "I'll have to shake that out before it melts." he thought. "Wet clothes will soon turn to ice, and ice turns to frostbite." As he wriggled out the other side, he turned to stretch a helping hand to Sinter, thinking too late that he should have let her go first. As he did so, she yelped, and seemed to leap face first towards the fence, catching the wire in her fingers, her face crashing into the mesh. Then she dropped into the snow, clutching her neck.

"What is it? Sinter, what's happened?" Saker called.

"I don't know, I don't know!" she shouted back in panic. "I think I've been shot!"

Saker grabbed her hands, and manhandled her under the wire. Shot? In the neck? Surely she wouldn't be talking if that was so? He pushed back her hood, and saw blood on her neck. There was no question she'd been hit . . . but by a bullet?

"Can you run?" he shouted above the wind.

"I think so," she cried back. "I can't feel anything."

"We need to get ahead of them, get back to the dogs," Saker shouted.

"Saker, what is it, what's happened?" she yelled frightened.

"It's nothing. Let's get out of here."

They thumped into the remnants of their old tracks, as the guards emerged from the buildings behind them, heading for garages where their snowmobiles were housed. Saker pulled his friend by the hand, his mind sickening with a terrible thought. What kind of bullet leaves such a small wound from a direct impact? What horror might already be alive in Sinter's veins?

There were worse nightmares than polar bears and blizzards.

As they stamped the few hundred metres to where the dogs lay sleeping beneath the snow, they heard the distant roar of engines being revved into action, snowmobiles that could easily outrun their dog sled.

The dogs heard the furore, and woke with a clamour, seeming to sense some glorious game afoot.

"You left them tethered," Sinter shouted with relief. "Smart move!"

"But we're two dogs down remember," he answered. "They're going to have to run like crazy."

He leapt onto the back of the sled, as Sinter yanked off the cover and threw herself down next to Yantar.

"MUSH!" Saker yelled, yanking the anchor out of the snow, and lashing the reins as if he was spurring on a horse in a Western movie. The dogs didn't even need to break trace, they threw themselves forward with such force that the sled gathered momentum as never before. As they got up speed, the dogs' muscular hindquarters and shoulders bounced up and down, broad paws like snowshoes, keeping them from sinking. Behind them, white beams from the headlights of approaching snowmobiles turned the windblown snowflakes into dancing pixies and fairies. That illusion was destroyed by the first staccato rattle of gunfire, and the whiz and crump as bullets flew past their ears.

"Saker!" Sinter cried, from her place on the sledge. "I can't feel my fingers."

"Of course you can't!" he shouted back. "It's minus 30!"

"No, you don't understand, I really can't feel my fingers. And I can't feel my legs either."

Saker's blood would have run cold, if it wasn't already two-thirds ice.

"And my lips have gone all numb. Saker, my pulse, I can feel my pulse, it's getting slower."

Saker's mind raced. She had been poisoned, there was no doubt of that. Something fast-acting, she had been shot with something that had gone straight to her core. As he urged the dogs on, pushing them harder than he would ever have chosen to, his mind scanned through a virtual checklist of toxins the Clan had used. It wouldn't be synthetic, that wasn't their style. It would have to be something natural, a poison from nature itself. A neurotoxin; one that works on the nervous system, heart and lungs? Cobra venom? Scorpion? No, they speeded up the body's processes, sending the nerves into overdrive. It must be something that did the opposite, a fluid that slowed everything down until the heart just stopped.

Suddenly he was shaken from his thoughts by a volley of bullets rocketing past his ears. And then a snowmobile pulled level with them. He looked across to see the passenger on the back aiming his rifle towards him. He was mere metres away, and even at this speed couldn't miss.

'HAW!" Saker yelled. The dogs obeyed turning left, without any thought for their own safety, pulling directly alongside the snowmobile, the wheel dogs practically beneath the skids of the vehicle. So used to spending their lives almost run over by the sled itself kept them from panicking as it smashed sideways into a half-tonne of metal and plastic. The man holding the rifle was thrown backwards, and his bullets fired harmlessly skywards. The clash itself was nothing, but the driver reacted as soon as he saw the sled bearing down on him, wrenching the handlebars to the left, taking his snowmobile sideways onto the slopes of the escarpment. Snowmobiles are ridiculously powerful and stable when they're going forwards up and down slopes, their one weakness is being toppled sideways. The whole machine wobbled, then flipped completely upside down, crushing the occupants beneath.

"GEE!" Saker shouted and the dogs turned right. Their pursuers would not fall for the same trick twice, he needed a better plan.

As two more riders loomed from behind, his thoughts were interrupted by a sudden realisation. Of course. There was only one toxin that could have been used in the dart; tetrodotoxin. He had read about it, but never actually seen the fluid for real. Colourless, odourless, it paralysed, giving all the signs of a heart attack – reducing the vital signs of breathing and heartbeat, until eventually killing the victim, then quickly leaving the system, leaving no trace.

But it wasn't infallible. Like all members of the Clan, Saker had studied his methods with infinite precision. There was no antidote, but a story from the textbooks came back to him. In Australia, a bather had found a blue-ringed octopus and, admiring its pretty colours, caught it and posed for a photo with it sitting on her shoulder. She had never felt the bite, and fallen into a coma. Everyone thought she was dead, but the medical team continued to give her mouth-to-mouth and heart massage for twenty-four hours, effectively making her heart beat and her lungs breath long enough for the poison to leave her body. She had woken next day, as if from a deep sleep, but totally recovered. All Saker needed to do to save his friend, was to get her somewhere one hundred percent safe, where he could give her CPR for a full day, without stopping, and he might be able to save her life. But how could he do that, with a platoon of snowmobiles running him down?

Sinter's mind was racing too. Her body was freezing from the inside out, but it had nothing to do with the Arctic cold. She felt as though she was inside a glass box, she could see out, but felt disconnected from everything. With every breath, she could feel the strength leaving her limbs, and her breathing and heart rate becoming slower.

"Mustn't panic, mustn't panic", she told herself. "Just concentrate on breathing. How are we going to get out of this?"

The more she thought, the more hopeless it seemed. The town was several days away, even moving at top speed. The snowmobiles would run them down within minutes. What they needed was somewhere that they could go, where the machines could not follow.

"The lake!" Sinter's voice was muffled, as if she had a mouthful of thick treacle. Already her tongue and vocal chords were slowed by the effects of the poison. Her body might be shutting down, but her mind remained lucid.

Saker shouted at the dogs, and wheeled them even further to the right, towards the vast frozen lake that he knew stretched as far as the horizon. Behind him, he heard the snowmobiles closing in.

Snowy Owl found Wolf exactly where he knew he would be, trying to start the last of the snowmobiles in the garages in the main compound. The boy was frantic, and had over-revved the engine, leaving it sputtering and refusing to start. Snowy Owl reached out and took a hold of the accelerator, and Wolf's hand.

"It's flooded brother, you need to give it a break before it'll start."

"D'yu think I don't know that!" Wolf's eyes were red with fury, his desire to give chase overwhelming every rational thought.

"Take a deep breath, Wolf. Like you said, there are a thousand miles of snow out there. They can't escape us. Rushing off blindly will not bring them in any quicker."

"You're always two steps ahead aren't you?" Wolf spat. "I've let him go before. It can't happen again. There's no way I'm going back to the Clan without them. Or unless they're frozen blue corpses six feet under the ice."

"I get that brother, but right now, in these conditions, they have the edge. Perhaps it's just my totem animal, I don't know, but me, I don't much like trying to run through chest-deep snow."

Wolf looked at him keenly, Snowy Owl's reasoning had been right many times before.

"I hit the girl with a silver bullet. Packed with enough juice to bring down a bison. They're not going anywhere.

Pretty soon Saker will be pulled up, waving a flag, begging us to come and save her life."

Wolf sniffed, as if he had just caught a whiff of something delicious, his hot head cooling by the second.

"Maybe it's the whole 'owl' thing, maybe not. But if I'm given the choice, I much prefer to fly." And with that, Snowy Owl gestured over Wolf's shoulder, to a huge hulking metal shape, in dark green camouflage with bright red stars. As he turned to look, one huge rotor of the Chinook helicopter swung in the wind, a heap of old snow sliding off and thumping to the ground.

The second and third snowmobiles were no more than the length of a tennis court behind them as they hit the ice at the edge of the frozen lake. A rattle of gunfire was unleashed, but the uneven ground meant there was no chance of aiming accurately. The rounds whipped harmlessly past sending white geysers and fountains into the air. Normally the sled would have had Yantar's experienced eye to guide them across the treacherous lake, but this time Saker would just have to trust his own judgement. He knew the rules. White ice was old, at least a metre thick, and strong enough for a Sherman tank to drive over the top. Grey ice was less certain. It would take the weight of the dogs, and the sled if it was unladen. And then there was black ice; new, still forming. It might take a human's weight, it might not. Without doubt, it would not hold firm beneath a half-tonne snowmobile.

There was a yip from the front of his team. Topaz, his new lead dog didn't like the route ahead. He could sense the ice was thin.

"GO ON! HIKE!" Saker encouraged, driving him straight towards the weakest ice. Beneath the runners, they saw the change. Suddenly they skittered over sections that looked like dark glass, tempting, alluring, and holding great secrets. Snow dust raced over the surface, the black diamond ice was there then gone. Saker heard a creak, then a splinter, but in that same second, they were back on the solid white. The snowmobiles behind changed gear, and leapt towards them. A line of bullets sprayed through the ice alongside the dogs, panicking them into a sidewards leap, throwing the sled to one side and nearly overturning it. Saker pushed off at the last second, bringing them back to an upright position. Sinter hadn't even screamed. Saker looked down at his friend. He could just see her laboured breathing, as her lungs fought against the toxin that was bringing her body to a standstill.

"Sinter!" he hollered, hoping to bring her back by sheer will alone. "Don't go to sleep, don't let it take you!"

The black eyes of the lake appeared beneath the spindrift, and again he heard the tell-tale creak. Waiting till the last second, Saker threw himself off the sled, and slid across the ice, the sled and dogs racing on, without him. In an instant, the snowmobiles had eaten up the gap and were upon them. But Saker had judged it to perfection. The ice could just about hold a sled in motion without his weight, but it was nothing like strong enough to carry the two motor vehicles.

The first snowmobile disappeared in an eruption of water, swallowed as the feeble crust broke away, devoured by the blackness beneath. The drivers screamed in agony as their bodies were seared by the fury of the water, and they tried to swim for the edge before they ceased to function. The second snowmobile skimmed briefly over the surface of the water, before hitting firmer ice at the other side, crashing with the impact of a car driving into a wall. The driver was thrown like a teddy bear over the handlebars to knock himself senseless on the ice.

Saker found himself bruised, but alive, face down on decidedly thin black ice. Death cracks from the collision started to work their way towards him, with the pinging sound of slowly fracturing glass. Just metres more, and he would plunge into icy oblivion. He knew that polar bears could walk over ice like this, and they weighed as much as the snowmobiles. They did it by spreading their weight evenly on their massive oversized paws, and walking as softly as possible. Sometimes they even got down onto knees and elbows to spread their weight even further. Saker followed their example, shuffling cautiously on his belly, even when the fracture lines split right in front of his face. He had to get to safety. If he didn't, Sinter was doomed.

It seemed to take an eternity, but then, beneath his

gloves was grey ice. Reassuringly firm to the touch. He got to his knees, and half ran, half skidded towards where the sled had come to a halt, perhaps a hundred metres away.

Her eyes were closed, lips blue. Saker pulled her hood and dark hair aside, and pressed his fingers to Sinter's throat. There was no pulse. He had to start resuscitation, and soon. As he pulled her hood back into place, light fell across her face. He turned to the east. Through the whirling snow, the sun was rising, casting a weak light. He couldn't help her here, not out in the open. The only hope was their snow cave. He had to get the dog team back to the escarpment. Taking Sinter's cold face in his hands, he clasped his pink lips to her blue lips, and blew twice, watching her chest rise and fall each time. Then he pumped her chest fifty times, doing the job her heart should have been doing, driving the oxygenated blood around her body.

"You're going to be all right, Sinter," he said, hoping she could still hear him. "I'm not going to let you go."

He repeated the procedure, two big breaths, fifty chest compressions, then picked up the reins and shook them.

"MUSH," he shouted, driving the team back to the escarpment, and to the tiny cave that was home and survival.

Wolf nibbled his lip, his eyes darting side to side as the pilot flicked switches, talked into his headset, and ran through his pre-flight checks.

"Can't you just skip that?" he hissed at the pilot. Snowy Owl closed his eyes in embarrassment. Luckily the Russian pilot didn't speak English, and looked at Wolf not comprehending.

"Just a few minutes, Wolf," Snowy tried to placate him. "He has to do this, and as soon as we get airborne we'll be flying at a hundred miles an hour. The dog sled can only do twenty, tops. We'll have him in seconds."

"Not if the others get to him first," Wolf growled.

Snowy Owl saw then that this was an obsession, that Wolf's hatred was clouding his judgment. "Brother, you need to chill. This isn't helping. Holding on to anger is like grasping a hot coal with the intent of throwing it at someone else; you are the one who gets burned."

"Which retard said that?" Wolf snorted.

"That would be Buddha, brother." Snowy Owl responded.

Wolf's angry retort was drowned as the two sets of rotors on the huge heli started to roar. As soon as they'd reached full speed, there was a sudden sensation of weightlessness, the bird rocked forwards and took off.

Almost immediately, they were caught by a fierce cross wind, which threw the whole machine sideways, and jolted everyone inside. Seconds later they hit a patch of dead air, and dropped several metres like a roller-coaster. Their guts lurched as their bodies fell but stomachs stayed where they were. Wolf's hatred was abruptly forgotten, and he clutched the armrests on his seat till his knuckles glowed white. Even Snowy Owl's calm left him as the chopper was blown about like a leaf on an autumn gale.

"Is this safe?" Wolf yelled at the pilot. "You're going to kill us all!"

The pilot, his face set in grim determination, held up a stern finger to silence Wolf, He needed every ounce of concentration just to keep them airborne in the storm. The Chinook lumbered forward, a white wall plastering the cockpit windscreen.

Wolf squinted at the ground racing below. Snowy Owl had been right. They were no more than a few minutes from the base, and he could already see Saker's sled below, with the snowmobiles in close pursuit. As they watched, they saw the first snowmobile overturn on the steep slope.

"You idiots," Wolf cursed, then saw both dogs and mobiles break right and skitter onto the lake. The helicopter pilot turned to them and spoke in Russian. They didn't understand a word, but fully understood his gestures; pointing to the iced-over lake, he drew his thumb across the throat. "That place is death".

The drama played out below the helicopter, as if it was a child's game with miniature toys as the main characters. They saw the sled and two snowmobiles race onto the black ice, and then saw the two motorised toy skidoos plunge into the lake. They saw Saker get back onto his sled and set off again.

"We need to go down there," Wolf shouted at the pilot.

"Nyet," the pilot answered shaking his head, then motioning with a wobble of his hand that the wind was too strong to risk flying low. Wolf and Snowy Owl watched helplessly as the dog sled turned back towards the escarpment. But the plant had sent out two more skidoos, and within a few minutes they were on Saker's tail, buzzing like blackfly tormenting a grizzly bear.

Saker turned the sled, and drove it up the steep slope of the escarpment, trying to shake off his pursuers. The last two snowmobiles didn't slip off his tail so easily. The top of the escarpment was a thin ridgeline, like the tailfin on a moon rocket, getting higher and higher with only just enough room for one.

The skidoos and sled were forced to take up single file. As Wolf looked on, willing the Russian's bullets to hit their mark, Snowy Owl took his pistol from his jacket pocket, and drew poison from the vial for one last dart, which he slipped into the breech. He ripped off his seat belt, climbed into the back of the helicopter, and opened the sliding door. The storm outside was so ferocious, it threatened to tear him out of the door and off into the whiteness.

"DOWN!" Snowy yelled at the pilot, and then in case he didn't understand, pointed. The pilot shook his head, then gritted his teeth and started to descend.

"MORE, down more!" Snowy yelled. They were only a hundred metres above the escarpment now, which was growing into a sharp mountain ridge. Snowy Owl could see that the wind had sculpted snow over the edge of the ridge, forming a cornice, an unstable lip. To either side was a drop as big as a skyscraper. The heli kept pace, tracking alongside the dog sled and snowmobiles with ease. They drew closer and closer, Snowy Owl trying to level the pistol at his target, but at the last moment being blown off by the wind cutting in through the open door.

"Closer, we have to get closer," he shouted at the pilot. They were now no more than a stone's throw from the ridge. Snow was being blown skywards by the downdraft of the blades, leaving the dog sled at the mercy of a colossal manmade typhoon.

Just as Snowy Owl finally levelled his pistol on Saker, with him dead in the sights, Wolf realised the awful potential of the helicopter's presence.

"No! Back off!" He shouted at the pilot. "It's going to collapse!"

It was as if the mountain had heard him. That very second there was an awful crack, and the cornice simply disintegrated. The seemingly solid rim beneath the snowmobiles just plain fell away, taking them with it. Instantly they were overwhelmed by an avalanche, which, cartwheeled bodies and machinery into a billowing cloud of snow and ice boulders. There was an explosion as one of the fuel tanks blew, flames and snow blasted skywards, buffeting the helicopter. Snowy Owl shrieked, as he was thrown into the doorway, only just saving himself from pitching into a fatal fall. The pilot pulled back on the controls and lifted the heli to a safer altitude.

Saker's dog sled skipped, as a chunk of cornice fell away beneath it, slid wildly, then continued on the ridgeline. Wolf shook his head in disbelief; Saker had some kind of charmed life. He looked back at Snowy, who was also shaking his head; "I can't get a shot," he said.

But then there was another crack, like the sound of a revolver being fired inside a metal room. The entire ridge-line broke, like a section of a big bridge that had been dynamited. Chunks the size of houses tumbled down the vertical slopes, taking with them thousands of tonnes of snow and, as if in a terrible whirlpool, first the sled, then Saker, Sinter and then the dogs, pulled down by their harnesses and reins. As Wolf looked on, the whole team became tiny toys again, smashed in a tsunami. The howls of the dogs and Saker's screams were drowned by the helicopter, and the enormous avalanche.

"NO!" yelled Wolf. "He was mine! That kill was mine!"

Snowy Owl sat in the doorway in sickened silence blasted by the blizzard. Below billowing clouds of white swirled, tinged with black smoke from the explosion. Otherwise there was no sign of the victims. There was no doubt that they must all be dead. Snowy had avoided the reality of what they were there to do, and while he understood that the traitor boy had to die, had really hoped the girl might live, and was heartbroken to see the fate of the sled dogs.

Wolf was shouting at the pilot again. "We have to go down, I have to see him dead," he ranted. "And if he's still breathing I'm going to break his neck with my bare hands."

The pilot was clearly not prepared to risk the helicopter or their lives in a descent. Unbelievably, Wolf made a grab for the controls as if to fly them down himself. When the pilot took his pistol out and aimed it straight at Wolf, he showed no signs of backing down. Snowy had to step in.

"Wolf, they're gone," he said, pulling his Clan brother away. "No-one could survive that. She's pumped full of poison, they're both buried under half a mountainside of snow. As soon as avalanche snow settles it sets as hard as concrete, they're not coming back this time." He was shocked to see that Wolf's eyes were full of furious tears. "Not ever."

The Russian swung the joystick and turned the chopper

in a tight circle, back towards base. Both boys looked down to where the last few ice boulders were still rolling, and the fog of avalanche dust was dissipating. Their problems had all been buried. Buried alive.

To the two Clan boys, Hep's flashy apartment seemed even more incongruous after swooping over the endless barren whiteness, and seeing the power of the wild world outside. They stood beneath the creepy stuffed polar bear, waiting for Hep to finish straightening his tie in the mirror.

"They're gone," Wolf told Rylander. "We watched them get buried in an avalanche. I wanted to confirm the kill, but your helicopter pilot didn't have the guts to go down."

"That don't seem likely," Rylander countered. "Say what you like about these Russians, but they're made of rusty old iron bars. They ain't short on nerve. And the pilots are all ex-military. They're the best. Strikes me your fella must be good and dead . . . and that's what we wanted, right?"

Wolf grumbled his assent. There was too much history, too much bad blood for him to give up this time; not without zipping up the body bag himself.

"So I guess I owe you one there, pardner," the Texan said. Behind him Snowy Owl smirked. He couldn't believe anyone actually used the word "pardner" for real.

"Seems you probably saved my skin. Say whenever

someone does me a favour, I usually give them one of these. How d'ya like one all for yourself? Shot him myself last time I was out here."

With that he took a wolf pelt from the back of his couch. The silver fur was so beautiful; he couldn't help but run his fingers through it.

"White Arctic wolf skin like this is worth a small fortune."

Snowy shook his head. Seriously? Hep was offering Wolf the skin of his own totem animal. The look on Wolf's face made it plain that the gift was not welcome, and Hep threw the pelt back down on the sofa. "Suit yourself. You sure there's nothing I can do for you and your boys? Tickets for the SuperBowl or Disneyworld or something?"

This time Snowy Owl actually had to stifle a giggle.

"The Prophet will be in touch with you," Wolf assured him. "And it will be to demand a lot more than tickets to a funfair."

"I bet it will," Hep said grimly.

The following day, the storm had abated enough for the boys to leave the Yamal. As they boarded the helicopter again, Snowy took Wolf by the arm.

"You have to let this one go, Wolf. They're both dead, you need to forget it, or this hatred will destroy you."

Wolf looked back at Snowy Owl, ever reasonable, ever

the peacemaker and replied. "The first time Saker escaped, the Prophet took me back to the forest." Snowy instantly knew where he meant. A secret part of the endless ancient woodlands where every Clan boy was raised, trained, and lived most of their lives.

"He took me to a meadow grazed by deer. It was summer, so there were wildflowers, butterflies in the orchids. Birds singing."

Snowy Owl nodded. Places like that had been his home every day when he was growing up with the Clan. Then Wolf broke the mood.

"The Prophet told me that every Clan boy who had failed in a mission was buried there." Wolf stared into Snowy's eyes; his gaze was so unbearably intense that a lesser person would have been forced to look away.

"There were no headstones, no markers, nothing. Just grass and flowers." Wolf was the first to turn away. "If I fail again, there will be no second chances, no forgiveness, no comebacks, just a shallow grave. No-one will ever question it, no-one will miss me, no-one will ever know what's happened to me."

Snowy was speechless. After a minute Wolf continued.

"Every night since then I wake up expecting to see an assassin by my bed. This was my chance to end those demons."

Snowy Owl's mind raced to process what he'd just heard. "But he couldn't . . . I mean, we're brothers, surely . . ."

"Haven't you ever wondered what happens to our

brothers who never come back from a mission?" Wolf asked. "Or about the boys who ask too many questions, and next morning their bed is empty? Grow up, Snowy."

He shouldered his bag, and stepped in to the helicopter. Snowy stood for a while before finally picking up his canvas duffel bag, throwing it inside, and stooping to follow. Wolf's words rang in his ears; *"There will be no second chances."*

10

The old woman, Laisa, made her way slowly through the snow, her two dogs trotting impatiently at her heels. For the previous few days her family had been confined to their caribou hide tent, only coming out occasionally to check on the herds. The gale whipped the tent walls over and over, droning relentlessly in a way that would drive a non-Arctic dweller insane. The Nenet peoples of the Yamal however were so used to the sound that it was like a winter lullaby. They had muskoxen skins to keep themselves warm, thicker and more insulating than any modern fabrics. And they had muktaaq to eat; boiled whale skin and blubber so rich in calories that it kept their bodies going whatever the weather was doing outside.

That morning though, the storm had blown itself out, and the family had gone to check the area. Blizzards had drowned the landscape in metres of snow, but the high winds had blown some snow into drifts, revealing rocks covered with lichen that the caribou would be able to graze on. It had been a gruelling winter, and their supplies of hay were almost finished. Opportunities like that would mean the difference between their herd surviving, or perishing just before the arrival of the life-giving spring.

Usually Laisa would have steered clear of the ground at the base of the escarpment, as it was prone to deep drifts, but there had been a recent avalanche, so the snow was packed as hard as concrete; easy to walk on. She tapped ahead with her walking stick, probing the snow, making sure there were no nasty surprises. Her stick hit something solid. Perhaps a rock? She scraped away the surface snow to see. No, it was wooden! Laisa started with surprise. This would be something to tell to her family later that evening. And perhaps good dry wood for their stove as well. But what was it doing here? She dug a little more. With a shock, she realised that she was looking at the remains of a dog sled, and wondered if it was the cause of the avalanche. "Some fool trying to sled along the top of the escarpment, and it simply gave way", she thought. Should she go back and get her grandson? He was thirty-five years old and strong, raising two children of his own. He would be much better at digging through the compacted crust. But inquisitiveness drove her on, she would dig just a little more.

Her next discovery was a caribou hide blanket, which must have been covering the sled itself. This was really exciting – what on earth would be loaded on the sledge?

In her part of the world, everything, absolutely everything from the outside was more valuable than gold dust. It could be tinned food, perhaps an axe or shovel. It could even be a functioning rifle they could use to frighten off the polar bears and prowling wolves.

But nothing could have prepared Laisa for what she found beneath the blanket. It was a young girl, her face blue as the ice, lips purple as if they'd been stained with the blueberries the Nenet peoples feast on in late summer. Laisa's fingers teased back the hair from the girl's forehead, and gently opened one of her eyes, then recoiled. Her eyes were amber, like the big she-wolf that had roamed around their camp the year before. The girl must have been a real beauty in life.

Laisa's fingers moved quickly to her throat, and the arteries that should carry blood to the brain. She sought a pulse. Nothing. The girl was dead. Nevertheless, she kept on digging, releasing Sinter from her icy shroud. She looked as fragile as a porcelain doll. Laisa placed her hands on Sinter's temples and chanted a few short phrases, willing her soul on its way. But it wasn't enough.

She would go and fetch her grandson after all, she decided. At least they could give the girl a proper burial and ease her passage into the other world.

But there was another reason she didn't want to leave Sinter there on the ice. Every group of peoples living in the coldest corners of the world have known for centuries a simple truth. One that modern medicine is still struggling to understand. They know that extreme cold can sometimes be a saviour. That a person frozen in the ice may show no vital signs, but can be kept alive as if in suspended animation. In normal circumstances, no human being can survive without their heart beating and carrying blood to their brain for more than a few minutes, but in the Arctic the rules are different. A bat or wood frog may lie as if in a coma for the entire winter, its body temperature at zero degrees, its heart never registering a beat. When warmth returns, they rouse themselves from hibernation, healthy and hungry.

No casualty in the frozen north is truly dead, until they are warm and dead. With that in mind, Laisa began to walk back to her camp.

11

In an endless nightmare he replayed the chase over and
again. He saw the dogs straining at their harnesses,
tongues lolling, and flecks of saliva flying from mouths
bristling with glistening fangs. And he saw himself lashing
out at them, a demonic spirit with a whip made of fire
sizzling above their raised hackles. He watched as the
Russians were thrown from their steeds, except in his
dream they were not riding snowmobiles, but black horses.
The stallions were dragged screaming into the impossibly
dark waters of a sinister whirlpool, eyes wide and white
with terror.

He saw the flight along the mountain ridgeline, but in
his dream below them was a gale-torn sea, lashed by
storms, waves curling to meet them. The helicopter was
transformed into a mighty black eagle, screeching its rage,
wing beats creating a mighty wind. And then finally, he
saw the cornice collapse, and watched his descent in the

avalanche. The snow grew like a terrible fog, tossing the dogs, Sinter and himself about carelessly. Down, down they tumbled, cold, cold, so so cold.

The last image faded, to be replaced by Sinter's amber eyes. He reached out to try and help her but she seemed to roll away from him, and suddenly he could see her whole face, expressionless, frozen, blue as sapphires. And her body, twisted and still, frozen in an icy coffin.

"Sinter!" he screamed and was suddenly awake. His eyes opened, but the rest of his body was unable to move. Fear tore through him. He'd been entombed in the ice, only his mind left alive! But no, that couldn't be true. He looked up and around him. He was in a blue cavern, long, deep and thin. The only light was filtering through the snow and ice around him. He looked down, frightened at what he would find. The lower half of his body appeared to be buried in snow, but his chest and left arm were free. He concentrated on his free arm. "Lift one finger," he willed himself, "prove you can do it." He focused on the forefinger of his left hand. After what seemed like an eternity, his finger responded, straightening and curling again.

"Right," he said, this time out loud, "so we've got one player, any time the rest of you want to join in, you just feel free."

It took nearly an hour to get the rest of his fingers moving, after which, he fell into a deep sleep, mercifully without dreams.

When he woke again, everything was real. He was alive! Somehow he had survived the avalanche, and was trapped in a crevasse; a slash through the ice at the bottom of the ridgeline. He remembered being thrown free of the sled as it was dragged over the edge. Perhaps he had been swept inside the crevasse as the avalanche surged over the top sealing him inside. In here the temperature was only a little below freezing, and he was protected from the wind, which would surely have killed him otherwise.

It was a peculiar piece of luck. His legs were frozen into the snow beneath him, and he couldn't feel them at all. He must be suffering from advanced frostbite. The mouth of the crevasse was many metres above his head, and the walls of the ice cave were too steep to climb without ice axes and crampons. He had no equipment other than what he was wearing, the only help for a thousand miles would be back at the oil refinery, where the Clan were waiting to terminate him. Sinter was dead. She was gone and he would never see her again. His guts churned as he realised this for the first time. Perhaps it was no luck at all.

Saker had always been a loner, much like his namesake falcon whose tattoo he wore on his lower leg. But in Sinter he'd found a companion who somehow seemed to make everything make sense. Like a sister. No, more than that . . . a soul mate. They had just been starting on their grand plan, one that brought together all their skills and training, that gave life a reason and a purpose, and now . . . now he would have to do it all on his own.

Saker was tough, he'd always sneered at terms like "heartache" . . . until now. It was as if someone had grabbed hold of his heart and was wringing it out.

The temptation was to fall back down on the ice and let the cold overwhelm him, quietly and painlessly taking him to oblivion. What was the point in struggling? He would be dead soon anyway. But Saker was a survivor. He would not go gently into the night. Writhing like a maniac trying to break loose from a straitjacket, he managed to free his other hand, and get it moving again. His fingers were so numb that when he ran them over his face, it felt as if they belonged to someone else.

Over the next few hours, Saker had the strongest sensation that someone else was with him there in the crevasse. Another person, talking softly to him in the eerie blue half-light, telling him what he needed to do to free himself. The phantom voice whispered advice to him. "Keep your fingers moving, get the blood running through them, stop the flesh from perishing." And Saker listened, clapping his hands together until the blood searing into his digits felt as if he was stabbing them with knitting needles.

After a while he began to panic, claustrophobia rising in his gullet, memories of black caves and collapsing earth tunnels tormenting him. He frantically scraped away at the snow that locked his legs, but the voice scolded him, telling him not to sacrifice his fresh warm fingers. "Use your pocket knife, have something else touching the snow so your fingertips don't freeze again," it whispered.

Throughout the night, the phantom refused to let Saker sleep. "The temperature is dropping, you need to keep active or you'll freeze."

Every time Saker stopped to get his breath, it would be there almost like a ghostly shape at his shoulder sometimes taunting, "You're weak, you don't deserve to live. Why don't you just lie down and give up?" Saker's pride would sting him back into action, scraping at the ice till his fingers bled. Then as fatigue crept in and his head started to loll, the phantom would chant, 'Saker, Saker, Saker. If you stop now, you'll end up like Sinter, your flesh frozen blue."

"Leave me alone!" Saker yelled, and with a final wrench, he hauled himself free of the ice, and fell flat on the glassy floor, his voice a howling echo in the ice cave. It was then that he became aware of another howl beyond the crevasse. Not a trick of the wind, or the chattering of an imaginary phantom, but a howl from the real world.

Saker lay breathing heavily, his lungs burning with the fire dust he'd been sucking in as he'd battled to free himself. He could hear something moving above. He threw back his head, and let loose his own howl. The sound reverberated around the chasm, bouncing off the blue walls, humming like a crystal wine glass when you rub the rim with a dampened finger. He stopped, and the sound died. There was silence.

"What the hell do I do now?" he shouted. And then it started. A sound from above; scratching, scraping. Saker looked up towards the light blue glow where the ice was at its thinnest. He could see shadows moving. Without warning, a cloud of white dust fell. Then a gouge was scraped in the snow, and sunlight suddenly cut into the cave like a laser beam, bringing the impossible blues of the ice to life. He looked back up at the hole to see a black snuffling nose, scrabbling claws, and then a furry nose pushed down into the small hole, followed by two eyes, one iceberg blue, one amber.

"Yantar!" Saker yelled

12

All the dogs we share our homes and lives with, no matter what their breed from Dachshund to Great Dane, are essentially wolves. Modern scientists call the wolf *Canis Lupus*, and the domestic dog *Canis lupus familiaris* – the familiar wolf. They are at heart pack animals, and when they enter our homes, they allow us to be their alpha, leaders of their pack.

Even more extreme, when we give our dogs orders, discipline them and provide all their food, we become surrogate parents. Such dogs never grow up and remain as puppies, licking our faces to try to get us to regurgitate food, never wanting to leave our heels, and chasing the sticks we throw for them as wild wolf pups might practise chasing jackrabbits. These dogs never really learn the ways of the wild and they struggle to make decisions for themselves. Yantar was not such a dog. He was a leader, alpha of his own pack, and fiercely intelligent, used to thinking his way around problems. The one he faced now was the toughest of all.

His wounds were already healing, and his strength had returned fast. Husky dogs are accustomed to running for weeks on end, losing their fat reserves, getting to the brink of collapse and then recovering quickly. They're also used to sleeping under the snow.

Yantar had dug himself free after the avalanche had settled, and had been trotting around on the search for food ever since. At the edge of the summer treeline he had come across the brown huddled shape of a wolverine feeding on a deer carcass. The wolverine is one of the world's fiercest animals, and will not give up its prey easily. However, this particular animal had already eaten his fill, and decided that it wasn't worth facing down the snarling husky dog. Instead he gave a fierce guttural growl, letting the dog know he could easily win this battle if he chose to. The wolverine sauntered off, pride intact, allowing Yantar to feast on the crunchy carcass that remained.

Yantar returned to the scene of the avalanche to see if he could find any of the rest of the team. The stench of death was harsh in his nostrils. The wheel and team dogs had certainly perished in the collapse. For a few minutes he scrabbled half-heartedly at the snow, but dogs are not big on cannibalism, and he decided other meat would be much easier to come by. Just as Yantar had made up his mind to set off, heading south where the trees were and the hunting would be easier, he heard the sound beneath his feet. Curiosity aroused, he started to dig in earnest.

Yantar was used to digging through snow, but the avalanche snow had set hard. It was an effort to scrape away the outer crust before breaking through to the chamber beneath. He smelled Saker before he saw him; the odour of stress and fear cloyed the dead air inside the cave and came rushing at him like steam pouring from a kettle. As soon as he saw the form of the boy beneath him, he barked excitedly. A companion! Yantar danced from side to side, encouraging the boy to come and play, but got no reaction. Something was wrong; the boy didn't rush up to him to bury his face into his fur. He just made noisy man barking, but didn't move. He couldn't climb the sheer walls of the crevasse.

Saker for his part was filled with such emotion that the tears ran freely down his cheeks, quickly freezing into a silvery sheen. Just knowing the dog was there somehow eased his loneliness.

Yantar padded around the lip of the crevasse, occasionally going too close and having to scrabble to stop himself slipping in. He yipped and barked to Saker, frustrated, still eager to play.

Eventually, he couldn't hang around any longer, and with one last sharp bark, turned and trotted into the distance. Saker saw the silhouette above him disappear and shouted out in desperation. "Yantar! Don't go!"

Saker felt a million times more alone now and pressed

his face against the cold ice, sobbing. No more. He couldn't take any more.

But then the phantom's voice spoke clearly in his ear, like the voice of the father he had never known. Warm, reassuring, wise.

"Know this," it said, "when you first think you cannot go on, that there is nothing left, that you can only give up and die, that moment is when you are only halfway there. You have barely begun, your body has reserves even it does not know about. It's time to find what they are."

"Yantar. Come on, boy. Come back," Saker cried.

There was movement above. Yantar's black nose poked over the lip again. The dog had come back, and this time he had something in his mouth. Saker looked up as a strand of leather slapped the walls of the crevasse. The leashes! Yantar had brought the leather ropes that would usually bind the dogs to the sled, and had dropped an end to the stranded boy. Saker's chilled mind took a full minute to comprehend what the dog was offering him. He strained to grab the lines. What would Yantar do next? Surely he couldn't actually pull Saker up himself?

Saker weighed around seventy kilos, which any sled dog worth his salt could pull. On the flat. On a sled. Pulling up a vertical ice wall was a different story. If there was to be any chance of success, Saker was going to have to give his all to help. He took his penknife in one hand in a stabbing grip, and wrapped the rope around the other to try and haul himself upwards. "OK boy, let's see what you've got. MUSH!"

Yantar was not wearing a harness, but merely had the reins between his teeth. It was too much to expect him to be able to pull the boy through his neck strength alone. But even so, the husky dug in his heels, setting his head forward, trying to straighten his neck and drive forward.

As Saker felt tautness in the line, he swung his penknife into the ice, splintering the blue, anchoring himself in place. His legs were still useless, and dragged behind him. With his other hand he pulled hard on the leash. Too hard, he unbalanced the dog, wrenching him backwards. Yantar yelped, then set himself again, gripping with his firm cheek teeth on the line. Saker swung again with the knife, this time higher. He inched up the ice wall, the surface melting, easing his passage, and yet chilling the skin on his cheeks even further.

One more pull. Yantar was at his limits, effectively trying to pull the equivalent weight of a sled fully loaded with half a tonne of equipment, but on his own. It was a ludicrous task, but the people of the far north have been breeding huskies for over a thousand years for one thing. To pull.

One more tug, a frantic swing of his improvised ice tool Saker let loose a war cry, trying to centre his anger, sorrow, fear, loneliness in one more effort. The edge of the crevasse was in sight. No more than a metre above. Two more pulls and he would be free from his deep blue grave. Anchoring himself against the leash, he spread his weight side to side against the walls of the crevasse, and swung up, swung for freedom and safety.

The blade of the penknife struck slightly off true. The bullet-hard ice had formed over many human lifetimes, squeezed from ancient snow. It snapped the blade like a brittle icicle. The broken blade closed on Saker's hand, cutting into his flesh. He let go of the leash and the knife, and bounced down back into the crevasse, clattering to the solid floor. Yantar was unexpectedly released and lunged forwards. He turned back, hoping to find the human clambering over the edge and up to safety.

Saker looked up, dazed, blood seeping into his eyes. He couldn't feel the wound in his hand. The silhouette of a dog above him barked once. Consciousness left him.

13

The Nenet tent was made of the hides of ringed seals. They get their name from their fur, which is covered with circles, like the stains left after someone carelessly sets down their coffee cup. The skins were sewn together, and arranged over struts of whalebone in a classic tipi shape. In the middle was a hearth, with a smouldering fire sending smoke winding up through the hole in the top of the tent.

A young man was carving a walrus tusk with his knife, making a spearhead for hunting seals. Later, he would wait at the bearded seal and harp seal breathing holes, just like the polar bear does, possibly for several hours, until an unlucky seal surfaced and died beneath his harpoon. The two children were with their mother; one not much more than a babe in arms was trussed up in a vast woolly pelt, with only her chubby cheeks and dark eyes showing. The other, a six-year-old boy was playing with a wooden carved boat.

Two husky puppies were trying to take the toy with their tiny sharp teeth. When they nibbled too hard, the boy scolded them, sending them scampering off with tails clasped tight between their legs. Outside there was the constant "clock, clock, clock", as the two lumps of bone around every caribou's neck bounced together while they wandered. Laisa sat over the mummified corpse, wrapped in thick furs. She chanted an ancient rite, had placed two fossilised shells on the dead girl's eyes, and occasionally rubbed her temples with warmed whale blubber, infused with dried salmonberries.

Her grandson, Dani, looked grim. Like all peoples who have lived many generations in the Arctic, his face and features were broad, but his eyes were narrow and dark, evolved to keep out as much of the high Arctic sun and wind as possible. Today his eyes were even more narrowed. His grandmother's desire to always keep to the old-fashioned ways drove him crazy. Using good whale fat on a dead stranger struck him as a ludicrous waste.

Laisa sat forward, deep wrinkles etched into her face told of a life spent smiling. "Tyko" she called the young boy. The boy looked at his mother, who smiled and nodded. Tyko didn't want to go over; he was convinced that his great grandmother was some kind of witch; an impression only heightened by the fact that she'd brought a dead girl into their home. However, he had no choice, so he tucked the wooden boat into his jerkin.

Laisa encouraged the boy to come closer and lifted the sheet from the girl's face. Tyko leaned over, his heart in his mouth, expecting to see a skeleton writhing with maggots. But the girl was beautiful, black hair tousled around her forehead, olive skin, eyes closed as if she was sleeping. She looked like a princess. He reached out to brush the hair away with his fingers, then stopped and looked at his great grandmother for permission. She smiled and nodded, as if allowing him a special treat.

Tyko reached down again, and then suddenly recoiled, and ran screaming from the tipi, followed by two very excited husky pups. Dani raised his voice; "what are you doing frightening him?" but Laisa's raised finger was enough to quiet him. He and his wife moved closer to see. Laisa took a feather from her hair. It was one of the downy chest feathers from a King Eider duck, white and black, lighter than air. She placed the feather on Sinter's mouth, and sat back. Imperceptibly, the feather moved. Dani and his wife crowded in still further, then gasped. The feather elevated effortlessly above Sinter's lips, lifted by warm breath. The girl was alive.

14

Drip, drip, drip in the darkness. Raindrops down vines in a dank limestone cavern. Centipedes as long as your forearm crawling through the eye sockets of skulls of the long-dead, cockroaches feasting on the flesh of baby bats that have fallen from their mother's breast to die in the mud beneath. The dark walls of the cave loomed towards him, the thickness of the air choked him. Heat now, rising like the sticky scorch of a Turkish bath. Sweat gushed down his forehead into his eyes. Too hot . . . got to cool down, need to get rid of these clothes.

Saker tore off his woolly hat, and began to rip at his jacket. So hot, he had to get down to bare flesh, had to feel the cooling breeze on his skin.

"Stop you idiot." A voice scolded him. "Don't you remember this from your training?"

Saker paused, feverish. Was that the dog? No. The phantom again? Probably.

"Remember. The last stage of hypothermia?" it asked.

Saker's mind raced. Hypothermia – when cold completely compromises all the body's functions. First stage was just shivering, second stage was numbness, but what was the final stage?

"Concentrate!"

Final stage, final stage . . . of course! The final stage was when the brain's thermostat got so messed up that it mistook burning cold for burning hot. Many victims of hypothermia are found half naked, having thrown off their clothes believing they were cooking alive. Saker put his fingers to his forehead. He wasn't sweating, he was bleeding. He must have hit his head when he fell . . . And he wasn't hot, in fact his core temperature was probably dangerously low. Unless he did something quickly, he would freeze to death. The phantom had woken him just in time . . .

"Yantar!" he shouted. The dog had been dozing metres from the hole. He sprang to his feet and was there in an instant.

"Good boy!" he sobbed with relief. "Good boy. Come on, Yantar, I'm ready to try again, let's give it another go."

Again the dog disappeared, and it seemed forever before he came back, but he did return, once more with the reins in his mouth. He dropped the ends down. They were just out of Saker's reach.

"Just a little more," he encouraged. "I can't quite reach them."

Yantar backed up, almost to the edge of the crevasse, his back paws set in the ice right at the very lip. Saker would need to judge his first pull very carefully; too hard and he would pull the dog down with him.

Saker clutched the remains of the pocketknife in his hand. It wasn't much, but even a broken blade would be better than nothing. He swung, and it scraped over the ice. Swung again and it stuck. He levered himself into an upright position, and gently took up the strain on the leash. Bracing his back against the ice wall, he slid forwards, and stabbed the knife in a little higher. His legs were still useless, still unable to hold his weight. He stabbed again. Feet lifted off the floor, knees now against the ice. He drew in with his pulling arm. Yantar leaned forward and pulled. His feet skidded backwards and he bent his knees to ease the tension.

Saker stabbed once more, screaming with the effort, screaming at the walls, and at the phantom, "I'm alive," he yelled with every breath.

Once more he stabbed. It was the lunge of a maniac, a killer blow aimed at Wolf, at the Prophet, at Hep Rylander with his stupid name and his evil profession. He was close now, could taste sweet air and the musty scent of husky, and feel sunshine on his forehead. One more swing . . .

Yantar skidded backwards, losing control. Rather than plummet into the void, the dog let go of the leash. It fluttered useless down into the hole. The broken blade wobbled in the ice. Saker teetering, his life balanced on the merest friction. Below him his knees started to tremble, overwrought with effort. He was going to fall, then that would be it. He didn't have the energy for another attempt. But then hot breath was on his face. Yantar was there, reaching down to him. Saker lunged up with one hand, took a hold of the dog's scruff and pulled himself up, then crawled on his belly, until he was clear of the edge. He puffed, panted and sobbed while Yantar covered his face with a lapping tongue that smelled faintly of old caribou meat. To Saker it was sweet as honey.

For the first few minutes, the thin polar sun on his face felt warming and nourishing. But then no sooner had he got used to it, than his body became aware of the wind, and how chilling it was. Rolling over onto his stomach, he started to dig a bed, just as his husky friend would. Yantar realised there was a game to be played, and joined in, glad to have a playmate and things to do. Between the two of them they'd soon dug a shallow depression, and Saker hunkered down, safe from the teeth of the cutting wind.

For a few hours, he curled up in the foetal position, with Yantar at his belly, better than any hot water bottle. As the snow drifted over them, Saker buried his face in the dog's warm fur, and wrapped his arms around him like a child with a huge living breathing teddy bear. The big husky would normally have shaken off such contact, but seemed to sense that right now it was life-giving.

Next morning, the pair rose and shook themselves free of the white blanket that had settled over them. Another night without tent or sleeping bag, and Saker had survived. It was a miracle that he was not going to waste. Having got his clawed hands back he put them to use. Taking off a glove, he untied the laces on his frozen left boot, exposing the top of his sock. Ever so slowly, partly because he didn't have the dexterity in his fingers, partly because he was so scared of what he would find, he opened up the boot and slipped it off, then pulled off his sock.

What he saw made him gasp in horror. His skin was purple all the way up to his ankle, swollen, and shiny waxy in texture. His toes looked shrivelled and grey. He kneaded the flesh, but couldn't feel anything. Saker had never seen frostbite before, but knew the simple law. You only rewarm it when you know you can keep it warm. Just like frozen food, freezing, defrosting then freezing again guarantees the meat goes bad. Saker would just have to leave his toes as they were until he could reach safety.

His first priority had to be the simplest necessities of life. Shelter, warmth, food and water. He suddenly realised how thirsty he was. It was so easy in the cold to forget the body's need for water. Saker took a handful of snow, and crammed it into his mouth, swallowing it in big chunks, and instantly got an ice-cream headache. Seconds later he started to shiver. Stopping for a second to think, he came up with the reason. Next time he took the snow in his mouth and let it melt there before swallowing it. His mouth hurt badly from the chill, but at least the snow didn't melt in his stomach, bringing his core temperature down.

Having slaked his thirst, his next thought was food and shelter. He could try and dig up the sled, then he realised what else he would find; the icy corpse of his friend. Saker couldn't face that. Just as he was turning over in his mind the options available to him, a fur ball, still warm, was dumped in his lap. Yantar had been hunting, and managed to catch a lemming. Lemmings are small rodents that live below the snow in comparatively warm tunnels through the coldest months; sort of like a stripy polar hamster. Yantar must have punched through the snow like an Arctic fox to be able to catch this one.

Small as it was, Saker couldn't face eating it whole, guts and all. Instead, he used what remained of his pocketknife to cut down the belly, and spooned out the guts with his finger. Then he nibbled around under the fur, taking chunks of meat with fishlike bones. It barely seemed worth eating it at all, but before he had half finished, Yantar had deposited another, then another. It seemed crazy that there could be life below the snow, but everything here depended on the lemmings. When the lemmings did well, lynx, Snowy owls, Arctic foxes, even wolves and wolverines had boom years. When their numbers were poor, the predators died or went elsewhere. This year was clearly a good year, for pretty soon Saker's fingers and face were stained with blood, and he could feel life flooding back into his body.

Perhaps he didn't need to dig up the sled. Maybe he could just make shelter at the base of one of the trees, and manage to make fire the old-fashioned way. Trouble was it was nearly a mile to the treeline. His feet were definitely not ready for walking yet, so he would have to crawl on his forearms and knees.

It took four hours to drag himself to the trees. To begin with the heat rushing round his body made him feel alive, and to be warm for the first time in days was a fabulous relief. Then the blood started to move to his frostbitten feet. The pain was unlike anything he had ever experienced. He busied his brain with thinking of comparisons for the pain; it's like walking on hot coals, like stabbing myself with drawing pins, like tenderising my toes with a mallet, like having a thousand paper cuts then dipping them in lemon juice. This helped for a few minutes, then he'd have to lie down and scream.

Yantar followed the whole way. When Saker pressed his face into the chill, the dog would whimper, and lick at his cheeks until he roused and began to move again. One time when he stayed down too long, the dog even took the boy's hand in his mouth, and bit until Saker shouted "Ow!" and swiped out in anger. Yantar didn't care. Better that than let him give up.

When they got to the trees, Saker could have cried with relief. He crawled to a stumpy pine, and started to scoop out the snow beneath it. However, no sooner had he lain down to rest, than he started to shiver again. Saker remembered that the last time he had done this ,with Sinter, he had fire, and a sleeping bag and insulating mat. The best thing to do would be to get to the snow cave. And that would not be easy to find.

Saker tried to get his bearings. The ridgeline rose high above them up to a mountain peak that was now turning pink in the fading sunlight. Beneath it was a world of white, but there were low ridgelines, called sastrugi, running across the landscape in long parallel lines. These had been blown into position by the prevailing winds and were as straight and regular as if they had been drawn by a geometrist's set square. All he had to do was follow them for a mile or so, until he reached the exact section of cornice, and found the piles of snow they had dug out. Grimly, he set off again towards where they had built their snow cave, what seemed like many weeks before.

It was after dark by the time he reached the cornice. Saker started to scrape away the white shroud that had settled over it. A great smile split his face as his hand broke through and into the entrance. Grabbing Yantar by the collar, he dragged the dog into the Polar version of Aladdin's cave. All of their food was sealed in bear-proof bins; sealed tubs that kept all scents concealed from their sensitive nostrils.

With his fingers still chilled, he fumbled around as if he was wearing massive mittens just to get into one.

However finally one spilled open, dumping out some chunks of frozen meat for Yantar to feast on. Right now Saker could easily have devoured it himself, but knew that all he needed to do was open another tin, and he'd have chocolate, porridge oats and pasta. Soon he was gorging, cramming his face, feeling his energy returning with every mouthful. Hunger sated, he unrolled his sleeping mat and thick down sleeping bag, and settled down for his first proper night's sleep in three days.

Unfortunately, his frostbitten feet would not allow him that luxury. The rewarming of frostbitten flesh has been described as an itch so furious you might remove the affected limb with an axe to ease it. Saker tossed and turned all night.

At some stage he must finally have fallen asleep though, as some hours before dawn he awoke to the sensation of hot breath on his neck, and the noise of a big animal sucking in air, smelling him out. The polar bear was back!

Saker was paralysed with fear, he couldn't move at all. There was no bear spray this time, no rifle, nothing. The huge bear must only be able to get his head and neck inside the entrance and would have to strain to grab hold of him. Saker willed himself into the far corner, pressing his face against the cold wall. He could barely manage a whimper. All that effort escaping the crevasse, the long crawl, all for nothing. He was about to be eaten alive. Dank breath reached his nostrils. He almost fancied he could hear the saliva drip from massive teeth.

Then a wet tongue slobbered over his neck. It was Yantar! He was back from a night's exploring, sniffing tree stumps and hunting lemmings. Saker sat up and threw his arms around the dog's neck. The worst was over. They were survivors. They would be OK.

15

I t had been naive of Sergei to believe his problems would
end when the sinister young Clan members departed.
Everyone on the plant knew of the break-in. The word
was that it had been an attempt on Hep Rylander's life,
and most were a little disgruntled that it had failed. It was
obvious that the invaders had been environmentalists,
presumably reacting to the fact that the oil operations in
the Yamal were technically illegal. Every day Sergei rose
and checked the news and his emails, expecting the scandal
to have hit the national press, but there was nothing.

After a few weeks, the whispering campaign began.
Two men had perished in the terrible avalanche on the
mountain. Four more had been evacuated with serious
hypothermia, frostbite, or injuries sustained in the
snowmobile crashes. Whoever the assassins were they had
not been your average bunny-huggers, armed with pots
of paint and stink bombs. They had been professionals.

Where had they come from? Were they spies from a foreign government, experts at espionage and sabotage? Or could they be from a rival oil company trying to halt production? Whoever they were it seemed unlikely this would be an isolated attack. They would be back and the plant workers were uneasy.

Far from being cautious, Hep had become even more of a tyrant. He had not returned to America as expected, but instead stepped up work on the pipeline, increased building, and started drilling in places that should have been fully protected. The wolf hunt also took on new urgency. The bounty on each skin had been doubled, and Hep had decided not leave until his quota was realised.

Finally, Sergei knew that he had no choice but to do his job, however difficult it was. He requested a meeting with Hep, and met him in his apartment beneath the disconcerting snarl of the stuffed polar bear.

"So what you got me here for now, Vladimir?" Hep asked. "What is so darn important that you need me to stop everything for a chit chat?"

"Mr Hep sir, you must realise that everything is not well," Sergei began. "Since the break in, the men think someone is trying to sabotage us."

"Damn straight they are!" Hep barked. "I have five years' worth of work to try and do in six months, and you can't even do what you're told. Half you don't even understand plain English."

Sergei fought the temptation to point out that they were in Russia, so that wasn't altogether surprising. "I don't always want to be the one pointing this out, after all you are the boss, but what we're doing here isn't strictly speaking legal. The men know that without environmental reports being submitted, and word from Moscow, all of this . . . well, they worry about their jobs. Some of them are even talking about prison," Sergei said.

Most of Hep's response had been totally unprintable. "Who's coming to arrest me out here?" he yelled, his face going tomato-red, spittle flecking his cheeks. "This is the Wild West, I'm the law in this place!"

Sergei tried reminding Hep that he only had contracts to investigate the Yamal, not to start digging and processing. "Mr Hep, sir, if anyone from the outside finds out what we're doing here, there will be big trouble. These lands are part of the Arctic refuge. They're protected. The local people have rights."

"Protected my speckled butt!" Rylander spat. "This here is the end of the earth. We're bringing prosperity. They should give me a medal! What are you suggesting we protect? Mud?"

Sergei sighed. He knew what was coming next.

"If you ain't with me, you're against me. And if you won't let me get back on track, I'll find someone who will."

The following week a helicopter arrived with a foreman Hep had brought over from one of his many stations in Texas. Sergei wasn't officially told that he was sacked, or being replaced. He just came down one morning to find the new Texan sitting in his office.

This lanky, overbearing, man was even worse than Hep, mostly because instead of staying in a warm suite he was with them every hour of every day, like a mosquito taking his little nip of blood. Demoted, unappreciated, and now talked down to by yet another American, Sergei decided he couldn't put up with it any longer. However he didn't want to return home in disgrace, and still needed money to send to his family.

That same evening, a grizzled man wearing a musk oxen fur over his shoulders and a beaver-skin lined hat, turned up at the base. His face was ruddy from wind-burn, and his beard flecked with ice. He demanded to speak to Hep. Sergei was sure the boss wouldn't deign to come down, but he did. Even more unbelievably, as the trapper handed over his collection of five wolf skins, Hep slapped him on the back, and laughed with him as if he was an old friend. Then he opened his wallet, and handed over a chunk of notes that made Sergei gulp. He couldn't see exactly how much it was, but it must have been at least double his salary.

Hep's plan was to catch the wolves purely through playing the numbers game. He had so many people out hunting that it had to deliver results. Much the same as wolves had been eradicated through most of America by hunting for bounties, Hep planned to use his money to catch as many of the wolves as possible.

Many of the men sent off into the wilds were professional hunters. They would set up barbaric traps near wolf dens; rings of bait tied to fish hooks. They knew that the wolf cubs weren't yet as canny as the adults, would swallow the bait and be trapped there in agony until the hunters arrived with their clubs. It was the most inhumane of all hunting techniques, but the wild men who went off into the Yamal to bring back wolf skins thought little of such things. To them, the wolf was barely a living thing, its suffering was as inconsequential as the suffering of an ant to a toddler with a magnifying glass. Hunting was both their business and, for some, their pleasure.

Sergei decided to go out to the hunter's lodge one evening, to find out more about the trapping business. He found the hunters sitting round the fire. The most accomplished had the seats closest to the heat, and generally the longest and most tangled beards . . . They swapped stories of legendary mighty elk with antlers that could lift a car, of fishing for Beluga sturgeon with the black gold of caviar within, or of the bear they'd felled with a single shot.

One told a tale of coming across a she-wolf that had been trapped in a leg hold trap for almost a week before he had found her. She was thin and weak, but had attacked him furiously as he approached. They gathered close to hear how he'd sat just out of her reach, and taunted her as she leapt at him again and again, teeth clacking mere inches from his face. The others laughed uproariously. To Sergei, it made no sense. The trappers admired the wolves; their senses, their wily nature, their elusiveness. And they prized the beauty of their coat, yet at the same time, they considered the beasts vermin.

Their own anecdotes revolved around how difficult the wolves were to find; they were extraordinarily shy, rare, and no-one had ever been attacked. So why did they despise them so much? To this question, he could find no answer, other than that they had been taught by their fathers, and they by their fathers before them. It was a hatred that had been inherited, like a silver pocket watch, and never questioned.

After several evenings Sergei plucked up the courage to talk to one of the hunters. In a corner of the lodge was an old man who kept himself to himself, his hair snowy white, but eyes still bright, and sprightly of step. His spot was a grimy high-backed armchair with faded flower patterns.

"Why?" Sergei asked. "Why do you all hate the wolf so much?"

The hunter fixed him with a penetrating stare, then dropped his eyes. Silence. Sergei shifted in his chair.

Just when it seemed there would be no reply, the old hunter breathed out and spoke. "Have you ever looked into the eyes of a wolf?"

Sergei shook his head. He had not.

"Then you know nothing." The man sat back. Sergei sat for a few minutes. It seemed the conversation was over, so, feeling thoroughly humiliated, he stood to leave. The man's voice stopped him.

"Man sees his own past in the eyes of a wolf. All the things we want to forget. We see our savage history, and it makes us uncomfortable. Over time, humans have taken all the qualities they despise in themselves and given them form in the wolf. We make him a demon, though we know it is not really so."

He paused, staring past Sergei into the flames. Then he spoke again. "I remember when I was young like these fools. Young and trigger-happy. I remember the first wolf I shot. She was a beautiful beast, and died trying to protect her cubs. I cradled her in my arms as the fire went out of her eyes. I had always thought that fewer wolves would mean more deer to shoot. That if we got rid of the wolves then this would be a hunter's paradise. But when I heard her heartbeat fade, I knew that neither the wolf nor the mountains agreed with me. I got ten dollars for her fur, and I spent it on a bottle of vodka. I drank the whole bottle, trying to forget her eyes. It didn't work. It still doesn't."

"If you know all this, why do you hunt still?" Sergei asked.

"It is all I know how to do," the hunter replied.

Sergei had spent most of his life in the city. He had no

idea how to find a wolf den and, though he wouldn't admit it, was afraid of wild animals. He didn't want to end up as bear food, or to be torn apart by wolves. But he decided to take his chances with the traps and the trails; he needed the money.

Easier said than done. For his first few weeks out in the forests, Sergei spent every minute of every day believing he was being watched by a wolf pack, that they were stalking his every movement, waiting for their chance to pounce. Of course he had read the reports saying that wolves never attack people, but didn't believe them. Sergei was also a realist. Fur might be the traditional way of keeping warm in Russia, but the truth was that modern fabrics were as effective, and far cheaper. Thousands of wolves, and at least forty thousand Arctic foxes were killed there for fur every year; and why? The fur coats they supplied were neither as warm nor as cheap as the artificial replacements.

The snowy-haired hunter showed Sergei how to lay a leg-hold trap, how to hide it beneath snow or tousles of soft brown pine needles. "The wolf is wily", the old man said. "Smart. Smarter than you." He fixed Sergei with his bright eyes and might as well have added, "cityboy".

"You must completely hide your scent and any trace you were ever here." The old timer took a pile of caribou droppings in his hand, spat on them, and ground his palms together to make a brown paste, which he smeared all over his jacket.

"So I don't shower or wash at all?" asked Sergei.

"On the contrary," was the short reply. "You must wash yourself every day to clean away the man scent. And after you eat, and after you smoke. But never with soap, just cold stream water. And when that is done . . . " he wiped the spit and poo over his face, smearing streaks of brown across his cheeks to camouflage the sheen of his skin. Sergei's face wrinkled in disgust.

"Cover your footprints when you can, make no sound, travel through the forest as if you are a ghost." He took from his pack, the cold twisted carcass of a deer fawn, and placed it in the snow. "Then draw him in with rich smells, and the promise of food."

The old man bent to the ground, took some pine needles in his hands, crumbling them in his palms. The fine dust did not fall straight down, but blew faintly to the south. The air felt completely still, but there was an imperceptible wind.

"You have to know the wolf's mind," he said, pointing away from the invisible breeze. "If he comes, he will come from this direction."

Sergei bought and borrowed a few basic tools of the trade from the quartermaster at the lodge. A sleeping bag, radio, backpack, map, and an ancient rifle that he was scared would explode in his face if he ever tried to shoot it. Then the trapping tools themselves; archaic-looking lengths of wire, trip mechanisms and metal instruments.

He'd learn about hunting and trapping the hard way,

or he wouldn't get paid. The leg-hold traps were generally the old-fashioned "bear trap" style. Trappers would entice the animals in with bait, then the iron jaws would snap shut on a leg. Unbelievably, even in these modern times this was still the most popular way of catching wild animals.

Time passed and he caught nothing at all. But once he started figuring out how best to lay the traps and how to cover his traces, they started to have results. He would have preferred it if they'd continued to be a failure. The majority trapped animals he didn't want; deer, pigs, wolverines and foxes. Walking into the trap, he would hear their screams of fear, often disturbingly like the cries of a human baby. Then he would see the whites of a doe deer's eye, the frantic tugging to get away as he approached.

He would cheerfully have set them free, but knew they wouldn't survive with limbs broken and wounds festering. To try and free a wounded wolverine or pig would also be incredibly dangerous. Instead, he would have to end it, with a rock, or a bullet. Every other day he would reach one of his traplines, only to find a precious gyrfalcon, great grey or eagle owl tattered yet alive inside the traps. Sergei had no choice but to break their necks and put them out of their misery. There was no sign at all of the wolves, but he knew even when the traps did succeed and catch a wolf, it might be a week before he'd return and find it. By then the animal would be thin, shaking, terrified, driven mad with pain and terror. Some would gnaw off their own limbs in a last desperate attempt to be free. Sergei could see that this was senseless, wasteful and cruel. And it wasn't as if he was seeing abundant nature around him in the forests every day. The only wildlife he ever saw was in his traps.

When he brought this up with the snowy haired trapper, the old man simply sighed and gestured to the trappers smoking and telling tall tales around the fire.

"The Arctic, she is a very big place," he said banging out his pipe. "But she is brutal. In the winter, she is dark and cold and there is nothing to eat. In the summer, she is always light and you are bitten by the blackfly. And she is still cold. Not many can live here, neither animals nor man. We have traplines for a hundred miles in every direction. Someday soon there will be nothing left, and then . . . then we move on some place else until there is no some place else to move to."

"And what then?" asked Sergei.

The old man blew out a luxuriant cloud of smoke, a perfect smoke ring and shrugged. "By then, I will not be here.'

Two days later, Sergei returned to a trapline he had placed down by the coast, hoping to have caught wolves wandering the shoreline in search of fish or seabirds. The traps were spaced out over several miles, and had taken him nearly a week to set. It was with dismay then that he found the first trap had been sprung; mangled and unusable but empty, with no prey inside.

With disappointment, then frustration and anger, he walked the entire trapline, and found every single snare had been treated exactly the same. Sprung. And not as much as a lemming to show for it. He returned to the lodge, convinced one of his rivals had sabotaged his traps. However, as he walked in he could detect a different atmosphere. There was a tension in the air. Sergei looked for the snowy-haired man, but another man sat in his place.

"If you're looking for Eugene, he's moved on. All his traps were sabotaged."

"Mine too!" Sergei burst out. "Every single one has been destroyed. Look . . . "

Throughout the lodge the hunters reported the same. Weeks passed, and nobody caught a thing. The trappers were nervous. Hep would be expecting his pelts, and nobody had anything to give him.

Some of the hunters were superstitious. They felt as if they were being watched. As if there was a malevolent spirit paying them back. Some even claimed to have seen a wild man, accompanied by a wolf that ran at his side and answered his commands. They said the spirit was always there, like a ghost, always one step ahead. They called him *nompyak*, which means "shadow".

As the weeks went on the stories became more outlandish. Suddenly the Shadow was the ghost of a long-dead tortured Nenet herdsman, who sucked the souls from those who hunted in his woods. Fear began to grow. Fewer gathered in the lodge in the evenings, as more of the hunters quietly packed their possessions and left the Yamal completely. Sergei however was not so superstitious.

Eventually he spoke out. "It's one of those 'hunt saboteurs', an environmentalist gone rogue. Either that or probably just some other hunters who are stealing your catch!"

But out in the night beyond their windows, a shadow shape listened. He never came in from the cold, and didn't take respite from the hardship. While the hunters warmed their toes and filled their bellies, the Shadow was hardened in the forge of the Arctic chill. The door to the lodge swung open, throwing sprites of firelight across the snow. The Shadow merged into the forest. His time would come.

16

Spring arrived in the Yamal like a blessing. Nowhere is more transformed by the simple tilt of the planet and the changing of the seasons than the Polar Regions. The snow had all but gone from the ground, and only hung to the higher peaks. Sea ice had first loosened, then cracked, then floated away with the winds and tides. The tundra came alive with a whole host of ankle-high flowers, lighting up the brown earth with purples, yellows and blues. Even a few bees buzzed and butterflies danced between the hardy blooms, though far more obvious were the clouds of blackfly and midges that made every other animal's life a misery, as the females sucked blood meals before they could lay their eggs.

Everyone in the family, even young Tyko, was standing by a series of rapids on one of the many rivers that had burst into life, flooded with snowmelt. The river dropped in a series of rapids over big boulders, and the family had been fishing in this spot for generations. Each of them held a narwhal tusk. The Nenet treasured these unique toothed whales. Until a few hundred years ago, people from the outside world had believed the tusks from dead narwhal belonged to unicorns, The people here though knew that it was the male narwhales who sport a single ivory tooth that pushes through the upper lip, and is perhaps used for jousting with other males.

The Nenet fashion a ring made of walrus leather at the end of the tusk, and attach a net to that. Each member of the family stands poised at the edge of the rapids, with their net. Fish called Arctic Charr rush upriver to spawn, and at places like this would have to leap out of the water to continue upstream. In just a few hours the Nenet could catch enough jumping fish to feed them for a week. Anything they don't need, they put into a dry smoker – a tipi of pine branches with a smouldering fire beneath it. The smoke preserves the fish, and adds a delicious peaty flavour to the meat. When they can't find fish, the family seeks out nesting birds like little auks, and catch them on the wing, using the same nets.

It was Sinter's second fishing trip with the family, and she had proved to be adept. On their first outing, she had tried to show them Saker's method of catching fish by "tickling" them, lying on her belly and pushing her hands into the water to try and get them underneath a fish. However, she hadn't counted on how cold Arctic meltwater rivers can be. As soon as she put her hands into the water, she had leapt into the air with a shriek, as if she'd put her fingers into a fire. The family were rolling around with laughter for ages afterwards.

Sinter had totally lost track of how long her recovery had taken, of how long she'd been living with the family, but it must have been more than a month. She'd missed the arrival of spring as she lay recovering, but had seen the first proper dawn as the light penetrated through the walls of her tent. The young mother, Nanavuuq, Laisa and Tyko could only communicate by gesture, but Dani had been to a missionary school in Salakhard for several years, and spoke good English. He had explained to Sinter how they came to find her, and how it had taken over a week before she truly woke up from her deep deep slumber.

He explained what little they knew of her condition. That freezing cold can reduce the body's natural processes to such a degree that the heart is barely beating and breathing stops, yet the brain doesn't die. Dani could not have known that this allowed time for the terrible poison to leave Sinter's body. It had been a million to one chance, but Sinter was a fighter and somehow she had survived. She had woken confused and bewildered, but the kindness and care of her new family had given joy to her convalescence. Tyko particularly adored her, bringing hot soup, and sitting on her lap while he played with his crudely carved toys.

It was obvious to Dani that the girl – although still young – was carrying a burden. However, it was not his way to pry. Sinter, for her part, took her share of duties as soon as she was able, learning about Arctic life. As the short spring came and went, and summer set in, the family were constantly on the move, taking down their tent every week or so to move to better pasture. By day they would walk the caribou many miles, then tend to them as they grazed, watching out for wolves. By night, they sat by the light of lamps filled with seal blubber oils.

The men would make carvings, or perhaps repair parts of the dog sleds or reins. This was considered the most serious of all work. Dani told her; "A pack of sled dogs is like someone you marry, and who marries you. They all have names, and they are never human names. The relationship between a person and their lead dog is a pact, a deal." Sinter thought back to her own lead dog Yantar, and how he had offered his life to save her. It brought tears to her eyes, so she shook the memories away.

Meanwhile the women would work on the family's clothing. The chunks of sealskin that were to be sewn into boots were too tough to stitch, so the women would chew them to break down their fibres, making them soft. Cow leather would be no use, Dani explained, as it freezes in cold temperatures.

As the days got longer they no longer had to light the seal oil lamps, and by the time summer arrived the sun would not set at all, and it was bright even at midnight. This was the time of plenty for every living thing in the Yamal. The caribou would eat all day and night, gorging themselves until they had massive pot bellies which would stand them in good stead when the long nights and snows returned. They gave birth to their calves, which tottered around on spindly legs, before nuzzling their mother's bellies in search of milk. It seemed like just about everything was having its young now, when the warmer temperatures and plentiful food made the job of raising them easy. This meant the predators too. The wolves they heard howling off in the distance had dens full of small furry pups, and they needed feeding. The caribou were an impossible temptation.

At first the wolves would come under cover of night, but when there was twenty-four hours of daylight, they had to choose their moments more carefully. Their targets were the youngest calves, still too weak to run along with their panicked parents. The caribou had little protection from the ferocity of the wolf pack, other than the Nenet herdsmen who watched over them. Dani worked together with men from several other families, keeping twenty-four hour vigil. When they first saw signs of the wolf, they would rally the herd together into a circle, and stride around the outside, brandishing blazing torches. They kept the huskies on leads, or else they would dash off in attack, and be unlikely ever to return.

Though this was the terror of their days, the Nenet didn't feel any hatred for the wolf. Despite the fact that wolves had the very warmest fur, the Nenet did not hunt them. When Sinter questioned Dani as to why this was, he told her that the wolf was sacred, the "Grand teacher or sage". Many of their shamans had the wolf as their "familiar", the totem animal that protected them, and mirrored their spirit.

Sinter drew in a breath as she listened, then rolled up one of her trouser legs to reveal the tattoo of the tiger's head Saker had etched there so many moons ago. Dani nodded in understanding. Their ways were the same. He went on to explain; "This is the way of things, the caribou and the wolf are one; the caribou is food for the wolf, but the wolf keeps the caribou strong. He keeps them running, keeps them from getting too fat, and he takes the weakest of the herd. Only the strong survive, and that is why our caribou are such good animals. The wolf needs us, but we need him as well."

Dani had warmed to Sinter and seemed to treat her almost like a daughter. One evening as they sat gazing into the crackling fire he told her the following fable:

A male wolf that was only skin and bones came across a huge fat mastiff dog, powerful and handsome. With great respect the wolf asked him about his life. The dog proudly explained that he had as much food as he could ever want to eat. That he had a warm place to lay his head at night. "Leave the woods" he said, "your friends will starve to death there, come join us."

"What do I need to do?" replied the wolf.

"Almost nothing," said the dog.

The wolf imagined such happiness that he shed tears of joy. But then he noticed the collar the dog wore about his throat. "And what is that?" the wolf asked.

"This?" the dog replied, "this is just the collar I am attached to."

"Attached" asked the wolf, "so you cannot always run where you want?"

"Not always," said the dog. "Sometimes my owners need to keep me tethered close, but I barely notice it."

The wolf, however, cocked his ears, turned and ran off into the forest, and still runs today.

Sinter's new life had a simplicity that she liked. And it gave her a lot of time to think, to make sense of the last few years. She thought constantly of Saker. Of how he had transformed from a sullen killing machine into a caring, occasionally even thoughtful friend. She thought of their grand plan, of the millions they had tucked away in secret bank accounts, of all the things they had hoped to achieve. There were so many powerful people who made much money out of destroying the planet, their plan had been to redress the balance. It had seemed that together they could conquer the world.

Now, knowing Saker was dead and all their plans were for nothing, it was difficult, frightening even, to know how she should restart her life. The nomadic life of the Nenet gave her plenty of tasks to focus on, and allowed her to put off making any big decisions. For now at least.

It seemed obvious to her that the Clan had been following them every step of the way, anticipating their every move. The only way that could have happened was if their Vietnamese contact, Minh, had been compromised. Surely he would be concerned by now that they had not been in touch for so long? Sinter would have loved to contact him, just to let someone – anyone – know that she was alive, but their satellite link had been buried along with the sled. And even if it was working, she couldn't merely contact Minh. It would be too dangerous.

If the Clan had intercepted their communications once, they could do it again. Just letting Minh know she was alive might be enough to have helicopters descending from the skies. Her Nenet friends might be able to protect her from polar bears, wolves and the cold, but they could do nothing against bullets.

Eventually though, after one too many long sleepless nights, when the sun never set and she never felt sleepy enough to doze off, Sinter decided she needed some answers. Hard as it would be, she had to go back and find the sled. Most of the ice would have thawed, perhaps it would be uncovered? She had no idea what this would achieve. Maybe she would find the satellite link, and could resurrect it, perhaps even risk contacting Minh? Maybe she would find Saker's body and give him a proper burial. Whatever, at least she could have some sort of closure. Maybe some clue as to how to move on.

Dani, Nunuvaaq and Laisa sat in silence around the fire that evening.

"I need to go back to where you found me," Sinter told them. "There are so many questions I need answered. So much that I need to know."

Laisa finally spoke, using the curious language of the Nenet with clucking tones, and a multitude of sounds not used in English speech.

Dani translated for her; "No good can come of this young *Yantar*." The family called her "Amber" for the colour of her eyes. Every time she heard the name, Sinter remembered the dog that had saved her life and felt a stab to her heart.

"No good comes from digging up the past. Whatever you find, it will not make things easier. Besides which, the animals will long ago have found your friend and scavenged his body. Are you ready to see his skeleton feasted on by wolverine and foxes? You might see that in your dreams for the rest of your life."

Sinter answered; "I already see that in my nightmares. The reality cannot be any worse than my imagination. I would rather see that, than always wonder what happened. Rather that than never know."

Though they disagreed with Sinter, they did not try to stop her. It was decided that they would help her in her quest. Sinter had noticed that in all things, young people received an enormous amount of respect in Nenet culture. The children's education was quiet, filled with example. It would be considered scandalous to strike a child, as their spirits were not yet fully formed.

Children in turn lowered their eyes respectfully to their elders, but were given responsibility, tasks which encouraged them to aspire to behave like their elders. Sinter was treated as an equal, and her wishes were respected. The very next day, Dani packed two bags full of provisions and sealskin sleep bags, and they set off for the long walk to the escarpment where she had first been found. They took two dogs, and one of their most precious possessions; a shovel. Sinter's stomach lurched when she thought what she might have to use it for.

They walked over low-lying tundra for many hours, rarely seeing a living thing. However, as they reached the more mountainous terrain, they saw ravines where many birds were making their nests, busy now the time of plenty was upon them.

Suddenly, without warning, a bolt of lightning scorched out of the sky, and hit a gull on the wing. There was an explosion of feathers, and the gull tumbled to earth, clutched in the talons of a brilliant white bird of prey. Dani pulled Sinter onto one knee, so they could watch the drama.

"It's a gyrfalcon," he told her. "The most powerful bird there is, they will travel far out to sea, hunting from the

141

icebergs, and when they target another bird, they rarely miss."

Sinter stared in wonder at the largest falcon on earth, the true raptor of the Arctic, as it angrily plucked the feathers from its prey. She felt a pang in her chest. It reminded her of another pale falcon. Saker, the totem of her friend. Without realising it, tears started pouring down her cheeks.

They walked clean through the night of the first day. With constant sunshine their minds didn't want to shut down even when their bodies began to tire. They both wore traditional snowglasses; a flattened strip of walrus ivory, with a thin slit ground into it, tied around the head with a strip of seal gut. They were uncomfortable, but far better than the effects of constant sun, scorching their eyes. Many of the older Nenet had milky white eyes where the sun had burned them. Dani was insistent that this would not happen to him or any of his charges. Above the horizon, they witnessed what appeared to be shimmering castles, dazzling towers far off in the distance.

"Where is that place?" Sinter asked with wonder.

"It is no place," Dani explained. "It doesn't exist, it's a mirage."

"A mirage? I thought those only happened in deserts."

"This is a kind of desert," Dani answered. "The air is totally dry. Those are reflections from ice floes that are way over the horizon. The first white men here called them *Fata Morgana*, Fairy Morgan, after the castles that their

King Arthur's sister lived in. Some of them are so powerful that you can see three hundred miles over the horizon! Into another world!"

If Sinter had still had a watch with her, she would have seen that it was four in the morning when they came to the base of the escarpment. When she had been here before, the view had been hidden by the blizzard, but now she could finally see that it was a long ridge-line that started at sea level, but climbed abruptly towards a peak high above them.

"The avalanche was on the other side," Dani told her. They would have to climb up and over the escarpment to reach it.

When they crested the ridge, they got a view of another sight Sinter had not prepared herself for. The oil plant was the first view she had seen of the modern industrial world in months. It seemed to her even viler than ever. Tall rusting iron chimneys vomited black smoke into the clean Arctic air. Thinner funnels had blazing torrents of fire erupting from the top, burning off the unwanted gases to allow the pure oil to be prepared. The ghastly horror appeared to desecrate the landscape she had come to love. It was almost as if it had burst from the earth, from hell itself.

Dani stood alongside her with hatred in his eyes. He spat twice on the ground. "My father's father remembers the first time the white man came here," he said. "They came here to trade and they promised everything. We saw

143

such wonders. It was not surprising we gave them everything. They brought weapons we had no knowledge of; my grandfather held a rifle to his shoulder the wrong way round and pulled the trigger, nearly blowing off his own ear."

Sinter laughed despite herself. Dani smiled too. "They saw their own reflections in a mirror for the first time, and made the sign of the evil eye to ward off the demons they saw. Another held a ticking watch to his ear and asked if it would be good to eat." Then he was serious again.

"These people," he said pointing to the oil plant, his voice thick with anger. "They come here and take. They do not live here, their children do not drink from the rivers. Their fathers' grandfathers are not buried in the ground beneath our feet."

He turned away as if he couldn't bring himself to look any more. "So they don't care if the rivers run brown with their dirt, and that the air has become poison."

He nodded to a broad sweep of forest that lay downwind of the plant. The trees should have been green and lush, enjoying the short growing season. Instead they were withered and brown. They looked as if they had been set on fire. Acid rain had killed them.

"They will take everything from this land that we have lived on for so many lifetimes. The land and animals here are tough in so many ways, but in others they are weak. Drive a truck across the tundra, and the marks it leaves may stay for a decade, perhaps more. Fill the rivers with mud and the Charr will never return. Kill the wolves, and their howl will not be heard here again."

"And what then?" asked Sinter. "What will happen to you? Will you move on? Find another place?"

"They will not rest until there are no other places left to go," he said sadly.

"What about the city?" Sinter asked, but immediately knew this would not work.

"I have seen the city," Dani answered. "When they made me go to school there. Every breath of their air is like smoke in your lungs. The people fear to leave the concrete boxes they call home, because it is warm inside and they hate the cold. They cannot catch the Charr, or seal, they have never tasted real food. They don't know real hunger, but a person needs to hunger every now and again to know they are alive. They don't see that they are living in a prison of their own invention."

Sinter remembered Dani's parable about the wolf. About how it would rather starve, running free in the forest than live its life wearing a collar. She suddenly saw why the Nenet peoples respected the wolf so much.

"I would rather die than go back to that life," Dani said.

"But this is your land," Sinter said. "Surely they can't just take it from you?"

"No, it is not our land," he replied. "It is nobody's land. You don't inherit land from your forefathers, you merely look after it for your children. He pointed at the towers, and concrete horrors below. "They will never understand that."

Neither of them wanted to stay on the ridgeline for long. The view had made their hearts heavy, even more so as they began the trudge down, to a discovery Sinter was dreading more with every step.

The base of the escarpment where Saker and the dogs had fallen to their doom faced west, and so had the least sunlight through the spring and early summer. Much of it was still clad in snow, and the ice boulders of the avalanche were visible from a fair distance. As they approached they scared off a cloud of ravens and an Arctic fox, which was in the process of shedding its pure white winter fur in favour of a coat that matched the environment and temperature more. It looked surprisingly thin, the brown fur underneath hanging to its scrawny body. The birds and fox had clearly been feasting on something. A carcass. Sinter's heart started to race, what horrors was she going to find by the snowmelt?

It was one of the dogs. There could be no doubt. The carcass had been eaten down to bare bones, but the scavengers hadn't yet managed to chew through the reins that bound him to the sled. Without really thinking about why, Sinter unhooked the reins and the collar from around the neck of the dog. It seemed the right thing to do. The dog had kept its side of their bargain. The least Sinter could do was let it be free in death.

Her stomach lurched. Now that she was so close, she

wasn't sure she could face what might come next and yet she had to see for herself. They walked slowly among the boulders and the ancient blue ice, finding pieces of sled, and their equipment.

Finally, after an hour of searching, they rounded a rock the size of a bungalow, and startled a flock of ravens. The birds had discovered something revealed by the melt, a carcass that had once been very much alive and had found its final resting place here at the base of the escarpment. Sinter choked, emotion thick in the back of her throat, and looked up into Dani's face. He smiled, and took her hand. Whatever was there, they would face it together. Their approach frightened off the last and boldest of the crows. But their flight revealed something she could never have predicted. Not in a million Arctic summers.

17

Sinter's knees were frozen from kneeling in the melting ice for many minutes before she finally understood what she was looking at. The dead carcass being revealed beneath the snow-melt was undoubtedly an animal, but was way too big to be one of the dogs. In fact it was around the size of a stout pony, with thick pillar-like legs, covered with dense coarse red hair. The real shock though came as she moved round to the head end. The dead beast had enormous ears . . . and a trunk! She was shaken from her reverie by Dani's hand on her shoulder. She saw that he was smiling.

"You are truly lucky, *Yantar*," he said. "The frost gives up treasures like this only once or twice a lifetime. I have never seen one with my own eyes."

"But what on earth is it?" Sinter stammered. Her mind was racing. It was obviously an elephant, but how did it get here? It wasn't as if there were any zoos nearby it could have escaped from! And it was a dark shade of ochre red, and covered with coarse dark hair.

"It is a memory of the past," Dani said. "This land is old beyond time and has many secrets."

Sinter was flummoxed. The young elephant looked as if it had just lain down to sleep that very morning. It didn't smell even faintly of death rot. The ice must have kept it from the beaks and teeth of scavengers.

"But when did it die here?" she asked. "Before the winter?"

Dani laughed out loud. "Without doubt. Long long before this winter." He knelt alongside her and placed his hand on its massive chest, as if feeling for a heartbeat.

"This calf lay down in the snow at least twenty thousand years ago."

Sinter's eyes opened wide with disbelief. "Twenty thousand? But then, it's a . . ."

"What you call a mammoth," Dani nodded. "Every now and then the ice gives up one of its own."

Sinter ran her hands over the flanks of the young beast. She wondered how it died, pictured its huge mammoth mother standing over the body of her dying baby, cradling it in her trunk, trying to keep it up off the snow. Then ambling off to join the rest of her herd, mourning the loss of her offspring.

"I don't understand," she said.

"My people the Nenet, they first came here many generations ago," Dani explained. "When this land was full of mammoth, woolly rhino, even the giant cats with the teeth like walrus."

Sinter nodded, recognising the description of a sabre-toothed cat.

"The Nenet were new to these white lands, and didn't know how to live here in harmony with the animals. They were such good hunters that they killed too much. And unlike the wolf that only takes the weak, and makes its prey stronger, man took everything. And he killed not just from hunger, but for clothing, for shelter, and out of fear. The mammoth did not have time to learn, to adapt. As we moved through the North, the big animals disappeared."

Sinter nodded. It was an old story. As Clovis peoples swarmed across North America they wiped out sabre-toothed cats, dire wolves and ground sloths. When aborigines arrived in Australia, the two-metre tall wombats, giant kangaroos and perhaps vast lizards that used to live there, all disappeared. When people got to Madagascar they destroyed the eight-foot high elephant birds, and in New Zealand the similarly sized Moa bird, and enormous Haast's eagle that used to hunt it. The only place where big animals still roamed free was Africa, and that was probably because man had originated there over millions of years, and the animals had evolved to deal with him.

"What should we do with him?" Sinter asked. It seemed a tragedy that after ten millennia frozen in time, that the mammoth should become food for the crows and foxes.

"It is the way of things," Dani replied. "A sky burial.

He will be broken by the beasts, and his spirit can finally be free. His atoms will return to the earth, and perhaps in another thousand years those atoms will be a part of one of my ancestors."

Sinter blinked. That idea was a bit too big for her to take on board. She only wished that she at least had a camera, so she could show Saker . . . Suddenly she remembered how impossible that was, and the thought stabbed her in the heart.

They searched the area of the avalanche for several hours, but found nothing else of interest. The sled was beyond repair, though they took a few planks for their fire. They found the corpses of four of the dogs. Whether the others lay buried or not was anyone's guess. Sinter prayed to herself that at least one or two might have survived and were even now running free in the forests. There was no trace of Saker or Yantar's bodies, but Dani warned this was no proof of anything.

"Bears will cache their food," he said. "Take it away and bury it so they can feed on it later, and others can't find it. That's likely what's happened here."

Sinter nodded in silent disappointment. She wasn't to have closure after all.

That night in her sealskin sleep bag, and caribou fur bed under the stars, Sinter rolled around restlessly. Her dreams were busy with the images of huge red elephants rocking their way through the snows of the Yamal. Suddenly in her mind the mammoths were attacked by stick figures; as if Stone Age cave paintings had come to life. She saw the animals panic, trumpeting, running from the spears. Amid the terror she saw the baby mammoth, eyes white with fear. Finally its knees gave way, too tired to hold its weight. A single caveman stood over it, and took a boulder in his hands, raising it above his head to crush the baby's skull. His face was twisted in rage, with heavy eyebrows and hooked nose. It was Saker.

Sinter sat up, suddenly awake, breathing hard. She looked into the embers of the fire, and around them, half expecting to see wild beasts patrolling around their makeshift campsite. Dani was sitting by the fire, his shovel across his knees. In polar bear country only one person could sleep at a time, particularly now in the summer when any bears on land would be thin and hungry.

Dani stood, picking up a pan of herb tea that had been warming in the fire, and took it over to Sinter. Wordlessly he offered it to her. She drank, and then sat composing her thoughts. Finally she spoke. "Dani. That mammoth, is it completely dead?"

Dani looked at her quizzically. She rephrased it. "I mean, could you get anything from it?"

Dani cocked his head, like a dog waiting for a treat. Sinter tried one more time.

"Well, I've read about scientists, they've taken samples, like DNA or something. I mean, could you take a sample, and then clone it – I don't know, maybe put the DNA into an elephant . . ." She was thinking on her feet now. "You could clone the mammoth, and then maybe give birth to new mammoths!"

Dani was looking at her as if she was mad. Clearly his education had not stretched to *Jurassic Park*.

"But why would you do that?" he asked. "You would bring one mammoth back to a world with no mammoths! What would be the point?"

Sinter shook her head. "I don't know. I guess if we humans are responsible for wiping out the animals, then it should be up to us to bring them back."

"Or we could just not destroy them in the first place," Dani said simply. "If people think they can magic an animal back from extinction, then they have no reason to stop them going extinct."

"It's science isn't it? I mean we know better now." Sinter wasn't sure if she believed her own words.

"Man wants to control nature," Dani replied with distaste. "He wants not just to play God, but to be God. Rather than facing his own mistakes, he glories in his control, as though he is a puppet-master."

Sinter thought for a second. It was true. If science did bring a mammoth back, it wouldn't actually be a mammoth. It would be some weird laboratory freak. But something else Dani had said touched a nerve. It all sounded really familiar. And then she realised. When Sinter had been captured by the Clan, she had been drugged and brainwashed by their leader, the Prophet. This was a man who revelled in his ability to manipulate, who really did consider himself god-like.

She recalled with horror how she had felt like a marionette, her words and movements entirely under his control. He was a man who would not think twice about experimenting on humans, even on human babies. Despite the chill of the bright night, Sinter felt the sweat bead on her forehead.

The Prophet had talked to her of creating "an army of no more than a handful of young men that could bring down a nation." Of "taking one child with the best methods that nature and science can provide, and creating an assassin worth ten professional soldiers."

Sinter had taken that comment totally at face value, but now something was tugging at her imagination. She remembered the Prophet's frenzied excitement as he'd started to explain his plan, his talk of serums and potions, of controlling people through drugs and science "without morality".

He had been just about to reveal to her something huge, something shocking, something about how he selected the boys to be in his Clan. Sinter had assumed they were kidnapped when they were still babes in arms . . . could it be even more sinister than that?

It was the mammoth that had made her think . . . As she started to doze again, an image came to life; a scientist stabbing a hypodermic syringe into the wide-eyed, red-haired baby elephant. She saw the syringe filling with blood, filling with the essence of the animal. The elephant's trumpet of terror transformed into the scream of a baby human, a new-born in the hands of two scientists, their faces covered with masks and goggles, cradling the child in rubber-gloved hands.

The baby still had its umbilical cord intact, and its eyes screwed tight closed, yet the syringe was being held in front of him. A scientist gently squeezed the plunger, and a jet of blood fountained from the needle. A fine spray dusted the baby's face.

Sinter screamed, scrabbled out of her sealskin bag and ran off. She needed to be alone.

Sitting on the ridge-line looking down at the rusting towers of the oil plant in the midnight sun, her mind filled with horrid unsettling thoughts. Something about the Clan had never really added up. The boys had been trained with the finest methods known to the modern world, and had knowledge and abilities beyond their years. But it was more than that.

She thought of her friend Saker, and his totem animal, the lightning fast, dark-eyed Saker falcon. So many of his characteristics were more bird of prey than human; the way he would circle his head, just like a falcon judging the distance to its prey. Sometimes his instincts were superhuman too, his reading of the world seemed to be a step ahead of even well-trained adults around him. Then she thought of the other Clan boys and their totem animals. She remembered her fight with Death Adder, named after the fastest striking snake on earth. His fists had snaked out at her too fast for her eyes to register.

"Just like a death adder striking," she said out loud.

Bear, a boy who could be no more than fifteen years old, yet had the strength of two grown men. Polecat, a lithe, sinuous presence, whose eyes, nose and face were constantly twitching, just like the whiskers of his ferret-like namesake. And then with a chill she thought of Wolf, with his gold eyes and padding gait. Quick to bare his teeth, seemingly tireless. "He's not just trained to be like a wolf," Sinter thought. "He IS a wolf."

18

It had been a fruitless day in the pine forest. Every single one of Sergei's traps had been destroyed. Some of them hung from the trees like chandeliers, dangling in mockery. At each new site, he got more and more depressed; weeks of work wasted. On the third failed site, he put his head in his hands. It seemed as if the whole world was against him.

Taking off his hat he sat down and took some dried caribou meat from his rucksack. The carpet of pine needles was so thick that it deadened all sound. Even the birdsong seemed muted. Suddenly, he caught a movement out of the corner of his eye. He snapped his head around, snatched up his rifle. It was an ancient bolt-action Mauser from the 1930s, with a cracked wooden stock, but would still kill a musk-oxen or man as effectively as any modern sniper rifle. Another glimmer of movement, sprinting on the other side of him. He swung around, bringing the gun to his shoulder, staring down the sights into the woods.

A stick snapped on the other side of him, and again Sergei turned, rifle ready to fire. He stood, heart racing, breathing hard for perhaps a minute. Nothing. Cursing under his breath, Sergei finally shouldered his gun and took a bite of his caribou meat, almost as if to prove to himself that he wasn't scared!

"The Shadow!" he snorted to himself. "Stupidity."

Half an hour later, he reached his next trapline. It was one of the hooked rings designed to catch cubs. Sergei had no stomach for this method. Secretly the thought of arriving to find four or five wolf puppies hooked and helpless, whining with fear made him feel sick. And what good would it do? They were too small to use their fur anyhow. It was just a sign of how much Hep and thousands like him genuinely hated wolves that they would even consider using it.

What Sergei found was perhaps even more unsettling than hooked wolf pups; . Instead, he found a pine tree decked in a bizarre parody of a Christmas tree. The bait had been carefully removed from his hooks, and hung from the boughs of the tree. Instead of decorations, the hooks were fixed with various oddities from the oil plant dump. There were rusty tin cans, a broken high-viz helmet, a decapitated doll's head with milky glass eyes, and a single boot, all swaying gently as if they had only just been left there.

Sergei looked around in bewilderment, almost expecting to see some small boy and girl who had been decorating this strange Christmas tree, perhaps hiding behind a bush. One of the ornaments caught his attention. It was a carefully carved wooden bullet. Curiosity overcame Sergei's natural caution, and he plucked it from the wire to study it. On the base where the firing cap should be, was the burned image of a bird's head. He turned it in his hands, then snorted, puzzled . . .

At that second there was a rustle at his feet. He looked down in time to see a rope noose come clear of the brown pine needles, before a tree that had been bent in half under great pressure fired upwards, taking him off his feet and leaving him dangling upside down by .

Sergei set to shouting and screaming himself hoarse, expecting an icy spirit spear to pierce him between the shoulder blades. After a minute simply swinging, he started to calm down. Looking down into the pine needles, he saw his rifle lying tantalisingly close. He reached out, brushing it with a fingertip. He tried again, but this time only managed to nudge it away. Then his attention was taken by something so completely terrifying that he recoiled. Leaping out of the bushes came a huge grey and white wolf, bounding with terrible menace before skidding to a halt below Sergei.

It bared its fangs, dripping with saliva, and unleashed a snarl that would have turned stronger men than Sergei to jelly. Again he screamed in horror. The wolves themselves had come to wreak vengeance!

Tears ran over his cheeks, and he prayed to his gods, apologising for every sin, begging for his life. The mighty wolf's nose rose to meet his own. He wanted to close his eyes to avoid the beast's terrible gaze, but couldn't. The animal's eyes were hypnotic; one gold, one as blue as glacial ice. Just as it seemed the snarl would be followed by the snapping of jaws, and him being eaten alive, there was a whistle from somewhere in the trees, and the wolf looked round. It turned once more, reluctant to leave its prey, then trotted obediently to heel.

Sergei's sobs were running out of energy. Was he about to come face to face with the Shadow? Hanging upside down as he was, he could only see the lower half of this new foe. The Shadow walked barefoot even in the cool of the Northern forest, and his bare chest was smeared with dark mud like war paint. Whimpering, Sergei lifted his head, to look into the upside down features of his enemy. He flinched with surprise. It was nothing but a boy. Admittedly a hook-nosed boy with sullen brow, and dark eyes staring out from behind sinister war paint. And he was holding Sergei's rifle.

Saker suddenly understood what it meant to have boiling blood. His anger was so fierce that his ears and face felt hot, and that rage was ready to explode. This man would snag baby wolves on hooks and leave them to starve. He deserved to die. Slowly. He took the man's rifle, pulled back the cocking lever and examined the breech. A copper-jacketed slug lay there, lethal at several hundred metres. Saker rammed the bullet into the chamber. The hunter moaned in fear. The blood had flooded into his brain, and he was close to passing out.

Saker longed to tell him what he was going to do. To torture him with words. But he probably wouldn't understand him. Besides, shadows didn't speak. Much as Saker hated to admit it, this man was worth more alive than dead. Dead men tell no tales, alive he could spread the legend of the Shadow. Perhaps that would be enough to convince other hunters to give up. Saker studied the man closely. He was so terrified that he had wet himself. Nothing would ever convince him to come back into the forests.

He grabbed Sergei's pack, which had fallen to the ground. Inside was some food, spare rounds of ammunition and a radio. He thought for a second, then turned on the radio, and switched it to channel ten, the emergency channel. Then he walked back to the man, and grabbed him by the chest. Sergei squealed and shut his eyes, convinced his final moment had come, but instead opened his eyes to see his radio pushed into his face. And Saker was pushing the "transmit" button.

It took Sergei a few seconds to compute what was going on. Then he stammered; "The Shadow, he has me! I'm on the ridge-line twenty miles south of the plant, please help me, help me!"

With that, Saker shut off the radio and put it back in the pack. He stood nose to nose with the man, his eyes burning with hate. Sergei heard a snarl that was so primeval, he wasn't sure if it came from the boy or the wolf. It was too much for him, and he lost consciousness.

19

Belly tight to the moss, ears flattened against his head, Yantar inched his way forward, every sinew of his body tensed and ready to pounce. His profile was so low, it seemed he was trying to physically melt into the ground. Ahead of him, he could see the motionless figure of Saker, lying in a patch of spindly shrubs, also trying to become a part of the landscape. Between them, munching on clumps of grass was a female Musk deer and her young fawn. The fawn was only a few months old and still looked a little tottery on legs too thin for its body. It clung close to its mother's side, relying on her eyes and ears to watch for danger.

Occasionally it nuzzled at her underbelly, trying to take a drink of milk. The doe was not comfortable enough to allow the youngster to suckle. She could sense that something was not quite right and kept lifting her head, big brown eyes scanning the thin forest, ears turning independently like satellite dishes to focus on sounds.

The doe dropped her muzzle to the ground to graze again, and Yantar gained another few paces, his damp nose twitching with anticipation. Steady . . . They had approached this pair over the course of several hours with impossible stealth and care. It had taken a lot of energy to get this close, there was no sense in wasting all that work by launching an attack too soon.

A horse-fly buzzed about Yantar's eyes, but he ignored it. Then it landed on his snout, wandered around in a circle as if searching for a good spot, then slashed through the fur and into the skin with its lacerating mouthparts. The pain was like a white-hot needle, but Yantar didn't yelp. He lapped upwards with his tongue, but couldn't quite reach the fly when he wrinkled his nose. The horse fly sliced again, and started lapping blood. It was too much. Yantar gave a shake of his snout and sneezed.

The doe's head came up from the grass. Instantly she let out a whistling warning call then bounded off, white tail flashing, her fawn sprinting at her side. The undergrowth settled, and they were gone.

Yantar stood up, and stretched backwards, yawning with his eyes half closed. His sinews had been bunched and tense for too long. Then he trotted over to where Saker was kneeling up, brushing himself down. Yantar did his best to look like he wasn't bothered by the whole affair, but his tail was curled to his stomach, and his ears were back in appeasement.

Saker knew that he was saying; "Sorry I made such a mess of that". As he got close, Saker leapt on the big dog, tackling him to the ground. They rolled over and over in the grass, baring their teeth at each other, aiming nips at the flanks and underbelly. Saker got the big dog's ear in a play bite, Yantar bounded away, then back into his stretch position, before chasing round and round the boy in a circle until they were both dizzy, and collapsed in a heap. Everything forgiven, they lay side by side, Yantar licking the human's exposed hands, while Saker probed in the dog's ivory and slate-grey coat, picking out ticks and fleas.

They'd both got lean in their months living wild. Their hunts failed more often than they succeeded, and much of their diet was bilberries, lingonberries, cloudberries, rowan berries and whortleberries. And, now the summer was waning, porcini, yellow chanterelle, and under-birch mushrooms. They'd even eat the odd nutty-tasting spider and wild garlic. Meat was a luxury, and hence they thought of little else.

Despite having the rifle now, which could have made hunting easy, Yantar and Saker stuck to more pure methods of catching food. Somehow the rifle seemed to give them an unfair advantage against the other animals, and didn't seem right. Saker had no real issue with hunting for his food, despite the fact that his mission was to sabotage the wolf hunters. He and Yantar hunted to survive. They targeted the most common animals, and weakest individuals, took only what they needed, and killed humanely and quickly. This was the way of the wild. The way of every predator on the planet. Of course Saker felt a moment of sorrow when he came upon the still warm corpse of a deer fawn that he had himself killed, but it was an acceptable part of survival out here in the world's wildest place.

The poachers, though, were a totally different story. They killed for enjoyment, for sport, hatred, or for the fashion concerns of rich people far far away. They didn't care if their quarry suffered horribly, or if their actions drove a species to extinction. They would cheerfully kill an alpha male wolf, despite the fact that it would tear his pack apart, or kill a mother, knowing that her cubs would starve to death. In order to survive, Yantar and Saker had to love the forest. It was their home, and would only provide for them if they treated it with respect. The poachers on the other hand would take everything; hunt the forest dry of life, and then move on to somewhere else.

Over the few months they had shared together in the forest, the dynamic between the two of them had changed. At first, when Saker had been crippled by frostbite, barely able to walk, Yantar would sprint off into the trees, and come back bearing the small limp corpses of lemmings. They rarely bothered with the cottontails, which would scamper down their burrows, and were barely worth the energy of hunting.

They did, though, revel in catching Arctic hare, which didn't burrow, but laid up in flattened patches of grass called forms. They would lie hidden, flush to the ground until the very last second before sprinting off at great pace. The dog and his boy learned to stalk the hares from separate directions, one eventually taking position flat to the ground, and waiting in ambush. The other would creep closer and closer, before flushing the hare into the waiting jaws or embrace of their partner. It was a strategy that brought them close, each relying on the other for a successful kill.

But over the last fortnight things had changed. Though they still worked together as a team, Yantar no longer wanted to share his dinner. Now, when he crouched over the body of a still warm hare, its glassy eyes staring, still full of fear even in death, the dog would look up through narrowed eyes and growl from the back of his throat, flipping his top lip to reveal gleaming white fangs.

The first time this happened, Saker had been shocked and afraid. He knew what this meant. The wolf that had been buried deep within Yantar was growing day by day. He was asserting his dominance, showing that he was the alpha; literally the top dog. If Saker was going to maintain at least equality in their little pack, he would have to challenge him. That was not going to be easy. Yantar was far quicker and stronger, and his teeth could tear Saker apart.

So Saker had to wait for his chance. It came perhaps

a fortnight after Yantar's first dominance power play, at a time when the whole forest seemed to be against them. They hadn't eaten for two days and were both starving hungry. Every time they came to a cranberry or raspberry bush a bear or flock of crested tits had been there first, and had plucked every single fruit. Yantar got so hungry that he even took to snuffling down caribou and rabbit poo in a desperate attempt to get some food. Saker tried it, but it just tasted like soil! Finally, Saker tore up a line of snares that one of the hunters had laid out for wolf cubs, shortened the nooses, and placed them down a barely perceptible path in the forest; just wire loops, tied to exposed tree roots.

Yantar sat watching, cocking his head to one side in the universal canine gesture of slightly puzzled interest. Next day they returned to the spot, to find two jackrabbits caught in the nooses. Yantar stepped in eagerly to take his share of the bounty, but Saker crouched over them protectively, exactly as the dog had done, showing his teeth, with as guttural a growl as he could muster. Yantar stepped back, uncertain. He had never seen the boy behave this way before. He paced sideways up and down. The rabbits smelled so good, and he was so, so hungry.

Eventually, the husky dropped on to his belly and crawled towards Saker on all fours, licking his lips, offering a truce. The boy snarled, the dog whimpered. With that, Saker knelt down, and nuzzled one of the rabbits towards

Yantar, all the time knowing the dog could tear him to shreds. The dog gratefully took the offering.

Saker's breath caught in the back of his throat. Would the dog take the meal away, and eat it in private, guarding it jealously? That would have been the beginning of the end of their little pack. Instead, the dog looked up with his one amber eye, and tucked in, tearing at the fur to get at the meagre meal within. Once done, Yantar came up to the boy, wagging his tail and licked his face, in a puppy-like gesture that said; "thank you for feeding me". Saker returned the gesture, totally overcome with relief. Things were going to be all right!

Only once their bellies were full could Saker concentrate on what their next move should be. Destroying the traps was certainly helping, as was spreading the legend of the Shadow, but it was all small-scale stuff. He was marking time, trying to avoid thinking about the future – and about Sinter. Much as he hated to admit it, Sinter had been right. The truth was that if he really wanted to make a difference, he'd have to get back to civilisation and contact Minh. With his computer hacking genius, he'd be able to come up with something much more effective. Saker's plan had failed, proving that he was just a blunt instrument, unable alone to affect the powerful people who had control. Hopefully Minh could use technology to pinpoint the villains at the top of the tree.

Yantar was now sniffing round the rabbit fur Saker had left behind, searching for any tiny drop of blood. Then he looked up. His canine senses had detected something beyond Saker's perception. His nose went back down to the rabbit, but he was bluffing, only pretending to be interested in it, actually his senses were now on full alert. After a couple of seconds sniffing, his head snapped up, he leapt back a pace and then barked abruptly once, his ears pointed forwards, thick hair at the nape of his neck erect and bristling, almost like a lion's mane. Saker dropped to one knee at the dog's side. This was really unusual.

"What is it Yantar?" he whispered, stroking the husky's wiry scruff. " What do you hear?"

Yantar continued his deep rumbling growl. Saker knew that if the dog had sensed food, he would have fallen silent, allowing them to begin stalking. And if it was a human, he knew better than to bark and give the game away. In fact the only time he had behaved like this, was when the polar bear had nearly killed Sinter. There was no doubting it, he sensed danger. And not only that, he was scared.

Saker followed the dog's gaze into the shade under distant trees. The spruce were densely packed here, and let little light down to the pine needle carpet of the forest floor. It was as close to darkness as the North got through the summer. The husky didn't bark again, but edged backwards, a low, cautious growl building from his belly.

"What's got you so spooked?" Saker asked. And then Saker thought he saw something. Two golden eyes glowing from the gloom. Instinctively he grabbed for Yantar's neck as the dog leapt forward, but too late realised he had taken his collar off months ago. He clutched for the loose scruff of fur behind his head, but the dog was already sprinting, barking with excitement.

"No!" Saker screamed, but the husky didn't listen.

The wolf pack had sensed the rabbits in their nooses many hours before. Frightened rabbits make a high-pitched squealing screaming noise, which often attract the attention of predators. The wolves' natural caution had led them to keep their distance, to watch the goings on around the traps before they went in and tried to take a free meal. The increase of trappings in the area had made them even more careful when it came to easy food; three of their eight strong pack had been killed by traps and guns in just a few months, and they would not be taken so easily again. When the boy had arrived, they might have quietly slunk away, their presence never known or noticed. If it wasn't for the handsome husky that trotted by his heels, his two-tone slate-grey and ivory coat glossy in the watery summer sunlight.

Wolves and dogs may be so closely related, that modern science suggests they are the same thing, but that doesn't mean they make fast friends. Far from it. In fact, one of the reasons ranchers so despise wolves is that they are known for luring pet dogs out into the woods, before killing them. No-one really knows why. Perhaps it is a remnant of some ancestral hatred, the wolves recognising traitors from their own kind. Saker knew all this. Yantar unfortunately did not.

"Yantar, come back, it's a trap," Saker yelled in desperation, springing after the disappearing shape. To his dismay, he saw the big husky gallop off, leaping over the undergrowth like a show pony. One female wolf stood exposed in a clearing, tail wagging uncertainly, ears flush against her head. As Yantar approached, she rolled onto her back, exposing her belly and throat to the dog, the very picture of compliance, giving herself to him.

Yantar stopped nearby, and sniffed the ground where she had been lying. He could smell that she was receptive, fertile, ready to breed. The scent drove him crazy, there was nothing he could do to resist it, and he gently trotted in, nose close to the ground, sucking in stories of smell, learning about his potential mate with every sniff of her odour. As he came to her side, her scent was overwhelming, he couldn't restrain himself. He bared his teeth, in a futile attempt to show that he was strong, but the truth was that her perfume had made him weak, weak in the millennia-old desire to mate.

Saker ran, thorns and nettles tearing at his shins and ankles, shouting with every metre gained, desperate to distract the dog. Yantar was his Clan now, his only friend, he could not lose him. As he raced towards them, he saw the she-wolf offering herself to Yantar. But then he saw what the husky had been too intoxicated to notice.

The wolves all stood. They had been invisible, crouching

hidden, but now appearing out of nowhere, malevolent raging hell hounds, bent on primal vengeance. Four bristling Arctic wolves stood in a semi-circle, with Yantar at the centre. Their huge forepaws were braced forwards as if they were about to rip into a carcass. Like all Arctic wolves, they bore broad short muzzles, ears smaller and more rounded coats off-white. As one, they started to snarl. The noise reverberated through the ground, vibrated through Saker's bare feet, and into his chest.

Saker came to his friend's side to take up a defensive position. As he did so, the she-wolf leapt to her feet, and prowled behind the pair, completing the circle. There would be no escape, not this time.

Saker raised his fists. Why hadn't he brought the rifle? But the wolves were not there for him. Their target was born of an instinctive hatred, the urge to tear apart this canine spy, one who had left their ranks to nuzzle at the campfires of humankind.

The alpha male wolf, a bruiser who would have outweighed Saker, leapt in and snapped his bear trap jaws shut around Yantar's front leg. The terrified dog yelped in pain, and swung round to defend himself, but the alpha had already leapt back. As soon as Yantar's attention was turned to the right, another wolf came in from the left, and clicked his teeth around Yantar's tail, dragging him backwards and off his feet. As the husky came around and lunged for his tormentor, another wolf thrust in from his blind side, body-checking him and knocking him off his feet. Two wolves jumped forward and savaged his exposed throat.

"You can't have him!" Saker yelled, and swung a big kick at the dervishes tearing into the fur and flesh of his only living companion. The kick hit home, but the wolf was already moving. As Yantar rolled to his feet, his eyes white with terror, blood running through the fur around his throat, the next two attacks came from opposite directions. Saker dived into the path of one of the assailants, grabbing her around the legs and throwing her over on to her belly. This left Yantar free to face his attacker, and the two reared on their hind legs, locked in a fierce embrace, slashing at each other's lips and tongues as they snapped and snarled.

Yantar bested his attacker, who raced away yelping, face slashed by the big husky's busy canines. But then the next wolf sniped in, and the next and the next, until Yantar was buried beneath a seething mess of fur and white fangs. Saker waded in, hauling off one savage beast after another. They didn't bite the human, they just slunk away, then launched another sneaky attack when he turned his back.

Saker reached down, grabbed a she-wolf by the tail, and hauled her backwards, tossing her like an Olympic hammer thrower. He felt hot breath on his neck, and spun. The alpha launched towards him, a mass of muscle and fur, finger-length fangs bared and aimed at Saker's throat. Saker threw up his forearm as the alpha's jaws clicked together, millimetres from his face. The brawn of the alpha had been brought up short by Yantar, who had thrown aside two assailants, and lunged in defence of the human, grabbing hold of the alpha's foreleg. The huge male landed with a thump, sending up clouds of dust from rotting pine needles. The second he was down, he turned on Yantar.

Yet again Yantar had saved Saker's life, but this time at considerable cost to himself. He couldn't endure much more of this punishment. The gun may have been far away, but Saker could surely find some human advantage to the situation? Out of the corner of his eye at the edge of the clearing, he saw a stout dead branch, ran to it, and brandished his new weapon at his slavering foes. He crashed the bough over one wolf's skull. He swung the branch around the pack wildly. Eventually, the wolves sprang back, and only Yantar was left, bloodied, muddied, one ear torn near off, his face opened up to the bone and down to his one ice-blue eye.

The husky panted, drool dripping from his bleeding lips as he regained his footing and, wavering, he stood once more. Saker's breath caught in his throat. His brave friend had faced down five wolves, every one his equal and was still alive, still standing. The wolves were back in a semi-circle, eyes and noses down, legs braced, hackles raised and bristling. And then, as if on a secret signal, they turned and bounded away, just like a Labrador will run from its owner, pleading with them to play. Saker watched astounded. Why would the wolves run?

Yantar stared at the wolf pack as they disappeared,

panting furiously, then took a pace forwards his paw held bent, poised. Saker could do nothing, but watch in horror, as the husky took another step, then sprinted after them.

The urge to give chase is so deeply engrained in dogs and wolves that it cannot be trained away or overwhelmed by orders; that predatory need to sprint after something else that is fleeing is too powerful, whether it is play or prey.

"Yantar!" Saker shouted. "What are you doing? Yantar!"

But the dog was gone. Seconds later, Saker stood in horrified silence, as the snarls, yelps and screams started again, but this time far in the distance. He took to his heels, and ran towards the sounds, but by the time he reached them, the piercing squeals were all done.

The forest fell silent. At its centre, a slate-grey and white woolly shape, its purity stained wine-red. Saker didn't need to take a pulse. He knew. Kneeling alongside his dead friend, his fingertips gently closed the open eyelids, covering for the last time the amber and ice-blue eyes. His tears streamed down his cheeks and dripped onto Yantar's warm fur. The last rays of the midnight sun cut in beams through the trees, set alight by the airborne dust, driven into the air from the final battle. That night would be the first when the sun would set and dark would return to the North. Saker got to his feet. Alone.

There was no real reason for his next action, other than a deep sense of loneliness, the desperate, lonely feeling that he had nowhere else to go. He bent down, so his fingers traced the shape of the big alpha wolf's tracks in the mud. Then, stopping only to recover his pack, and the precious but unused rifle, he set off in the direction of the tracks, which led, like a broken promise, into the forest.

20

The clock, clock of old bone rattling on old bone had become like a strange lullaby to Sinter. If it wasn't for the annoying, persistent blackfly that followed her caribou herd, that lullaby would probably have sung her off to sleep. Minding the herd was generally quite a dull job; they really didn't do much, except munch at the meagre grass and lichen with a rather dopey look on their faces.

The boredom of her days was now tempered by the fact that summer had passed, and the time of the midnight sun was over. At the end of every day was a short night, and that was when they had to be vigilant. That was when the two clocking bones around the caribou's neck would come into their own, allowing the Nenet to keep track of their charges by sound. For night was when the wolves came.

The first time they attacked, Sinter was totally

unprepared. They had picked out a calf that had strayed a little too far from its mother, but rather than rushing in on the youngster directly, they attacked the whole herd from all sides, causing panic. The herd stampeded, Sinter ran with them, yelling at the attackers, swinging her blazing firebrand towards the canine shapes as they leapt towards her charges. Their eyes seemed to burn, their teeth to shine unnaturally white in their muzzles.

The wolves drove the caribou into a river valley with boggy ground that slowed some of them down, splitting them up, making it easier to isolate the calf. When Sinter caught up with them, it was too late. The mother caribou was bellowing with distress. The calf was nowhere to be seen.

When Sinter returned to the tents, she expected the Nenet family to be upset, even angry with her for failing to protect the caribou, but they had seen this drama play out a thousand times. Instead they took Sinter inside, and fed her a good meal of seasoned Arctic Charr cooked in whortleberries, and served with a tuber that tasted very like potato. Every one of the men took turns to serve her food and drink. They wanted to show their gratitude, and that they respected her bravery. Sinter felt like a fraud – after all, the wolves had taken a caribou calf on her watch. However, she was tired and hungry, and took the offerings with gratitude.

Next morning, Dani had led her over the tundra towards a valley. From a distance they could see that big black raven had gathered on every available boulder, evidently awaiting a meal. The last few hundred metres Dani and Sinter approached on their bellies, inching along painfully slowly so as not to frighten the birds, and hence warn the wolves that they were watching. The wolves had already stripped most of the reindeer calf carcass to the bone, and were gathered around the bloody skeleton playing, their muzzles stained with blood.

Despite her initial anger at the predators that had stolen her caribou, Sinter's breath caught in her throat with delight. The wolves had cubs with them. No more than two or three months old the puppies were round bundles of energy, leaping all over their mothers and their siblings, latching their teeth into the big alpha's tail and using it like a swing, until he turned and batted them down, then licked them over and over, like any proud father bathing their baby.

Dani didn't speak a word as they watched the pack playing on the hillside. He waited till they had retreated and were some miles away before he spoke. "The wolf's hearing is so acute that they can hear their prey's heart beating. When they hear the heart rate going as high as it can, that's when they attack; when the prey is most terrified. With hearing like that, they would certainly have heard us whispering even at a great distance."

"You respect them don't you?" Sinter asked.

"It's more than that," he replied. "We Nenet are hunters, and the wolf is the finest of all hunters in the

Arctic. In the winter, when they stalk the caribou I have seen them take mouthfuls of snow, so their breath doesn't steam in the cold, which might otherwise give them away. When they approach their prey, they don't just come from downwind, but they anticipate how the wind might change. Sometimes they'll wait all day for the wind to be right before they attack. Generations of my people have watched the wolf, and learned from him. We would never have survived here without learning his ways."

Next time she was on watch, and sensed the wolves approaching in the night, Sinter acted differently. This time she ran to the youngest calf, driving it to its mother's side. She then took up a bugle that had been fashioned from the horn of musk oxen, and blew into it, a clarion call to the other Nenet that she needed their help. The Nenet men arrived as fast as they could run brandishing torches, and surrounded the herd, preventing a stampede. The wolves danced in to the blazing light, showing themselves for mere seconds before retreating to the shadows.

However, they soon saw that it was a fight fraught with risk, and that they should rather go hungry than lose another of their pack. They slunk off in in search of rabbit, or perhaps a feathered ptarmigan, to sate their appetites.

As the wolves blended into the night, like the dwindling smoke from a spent match, Sinter fancied she saw another shadow moving beyond the dancing light of her firebrand.

This shape though stood upright, tall and slender on two legs. Before she could shout out, it was gone.

Later, back in the tents, she questioned Dani as to what it might have been.

"The caribou follow us," Dani explained. "The wolves follow the caribou, the raven track the wolves, and dead-eyed men with rifles and traps follow the raven, as they know they'll lead them to the wolf." He paused. "But these last few moons, the poachers have not had things all their own way. Their traps are being twisted and taken, and when I read the stories in their prints, I see they are running scared. There is something else trailing the wolves too. It is very strange, but many strange things happen these days."

In the morning, Sinter headed to where the unsuccessful ambush had taken place. She paced around eyes down to the ground, reading the signs as Saker had taught her. Most of the ground had been flattened by the cloven hooves of the caribou, their prints as round as saucers. Here and there she saw the flat imprint of the sealskin boots worn by the Nenet, as they'd gathered around the caribou trying to protect them.

Outside the ring of fire created by her fellow herders, she found a soft muddy bank, and here were the prints of the alpha wolf. They were huge; broad and showed the hairs between the toes that kept his feet warm. And there, just beyond where the wolves had been, there she found her prize. There was only one print, its toes and forefoot pressed deep into the ground showing that the owner had been sprinting, and was light on their feet. It was clearly human, because the runner had been barefoot.

As her fingers traced the edge of the footprint, a shadow fell across her. She glanced up, to see a lithe figure looking down at her, silhouetted against the low polar sun. He stood bare-chested and barefoot, even there on the tundra.

"Hello Tigress," he said.

21

For the first ten minutes they embraced, cried, laughed, and stroked each other's tear-stained cheeks, as if to prove the flesh was real. It was some time though before they could begin to speak. What can your first words be to a dear friend you had given up for dead?

Finally, Sinter asked the obvious questions; "What happened to you? Where have you been?"

Saker began to gabble the story of the past few months, of the ice cave, and his descent into madness. But after a few sentences, his overwhelming need to hear the same answers from Sinter broke his concentration. It was a fiercely emotional reunion, neither quite able to believe that the moment could be real.

When Sinter heard that Yantar had survived the avalanche, her joy and excitement brought Saker back to reality.

"Where is he? When can I see him?"

Saker looked at the ground. "He saved me from the ice cave, and kept me alive for that first month while my frostbite healed. He'd go out hunting hares and lemming, and bring them back to me."

Saker decided to leave out the bit about how the dog had then tried to assert his dominance over him. He saw no need to sully Yantar's memory. And besides, he had other demons to deal with. "But when it came down to it, I couldn't save him."

He told her then of the wolves, of how they had tempted Yantar to his doom, and how ever since he had been following them, looking for . . . well, he wasn't really sure what he was looking for, whether to challenge them, or make his peace with the pack, he didn't know.

When they were done talking, Sinter took her friend back to the Nenet camp. The Nenet took Saker's resurrection with the same calm that had greeted Sinter's strange arrival in their world. They treated him with the same hospitality, feeding the boy who was near starvation, with huge hunks of seal meat, washed down with caribou milk. It was thick and clotted, a little like drinking a pint of cream. Saker hadn't eaten anything so rich in months, and gagged at the taste of it, but Laisa forced him to finish it. If it's good enough for the caribou to give to their calves, it would be good enough for this skeleton of a boy to put some weight on his bones!

Later that night, around the fire, when the family had

all put their heads down to sleep, Sinter rolled over in her sleeping bag, to look at Saker. His eyes were closed, and he was breathing deeply in his sleep. She studied his face intently. Reaching out with one finger, she traced across his dark brooding eyebrows, just like the black eye-stripes of his namesake. Then she ran her fingertip down his nose, curved and hawk-like. She had always thought his nose gave him a harsh look, but for the first time realised that actually, his features were striking, handsome even.

He moved suddenly, making her jump back, but didn't wake. She studied his face again. Even in sleep he twitched with energy, as if ready to leap into action. "Just like a bird of prey," she whispered.

It was too early to broach the subject of her theory, about the mammoth, and what the Clan boys might really be. That perhaps their powers were down to more than just training, that perhaps it owed a good deal to scientists, to manipulating nature, and other possibilities too sinister to even think about.

"There's too much falcon in you, Saker," she said softly. "It can't just be down to a name and a tattoo."

They breakfasted early with Dani next morning, poking the almost dead embers of the fire, nobody wanting to be the first to speak.

"So where will you go now?" Dani eventually asked.

"I don't want to go anywhere," Sinter responded. "You have all been so good to me, and there's work to do here."

Saker looked up surprised, but saw from Sinter's face that her heart wasn't in her words.

"You have already done much for us," Dani reasoned. "But you are not built to live through an Arctic winter. You were born in a different world. Where you were born the sun always shines. Here, we have four months where the sun never even rises. It is not for you."

Sinter's pride was stung and she was about to respond indignantly to the contrary, but Dani stopped her with a raised hand.

"Besides, there is far more that you can do for us, for our lands, and for the animals here, than any of us can ever achieve. You know about the outside world, we do not."

"It's true, Sinter," Saker cut in. "In the months I've spent here, I've probably saved a dozen wolves. If we get back to civilisation, we might be able to do something to save the whole of the Yamal. We have to think big."

Sinter looked between the faces of the two people who had become most precious to her. She owed Dani and his people. They had saved her life, given her a family, shown her a way of living that was totally alien. She had very few people in her life now, and did not want to lose any of them. On the other hand, they were both right. She could do more to repay her debts from outside the harsh world of the Yamal. Perhaps her fate was sealed the day she left the plantation back in India. The roll of the dice and turn of the Tarot cards had condemned her to a life without a home. It seemed she would always be a fugitive, forever on the run.

22

The only way to get back to civilisation quickly was to hitch a ride in a truck heading back from the oil refineries. They really had no option, other than to hike to the rough road, and try to thumb a lift. It was a crazy high-risk strategy. Two young people hitchhiking in the middle of the wilderness were bound to cause suspicion. They might flag down a driver who had heard of the two runaways, and could turn them over to the authorities.

However, as luck would have it, after just a few hours of waiting they managed to thumb a lift from a trucker who was running errands to and from the refineries. He barely spoke a word to them over the entire two-day drive to Salakhard. He didn't even ask them what they were doing, stranded in the middle of the tundra, miles from any towns or villages. Instead, he just offered them some meat dumplings from a Tupperware box he kept in the back of the lorry's huge cab, took another for himself, and kept his eyes on the road.

Salakhard City is not many people's idea of a modern metropolis. In the winter, it is dark and bitterly cold. Its concrete-box Soviet architecture is so lacking in soul that the cityscape seems to have been coloured by a depressed artist who only has shades of grey in their paint box. In summer, it is plagued by blackfly, so people standing at bus stops have to keep walking around in circles, flailing their arms to foil the biting menaces. It would have seemed a miserable place at any time, but after so many months free under the big skies of the high Arctic, it felt especially grim.

Once they had waved goodbye to their less than chatty truck driver, the pair sought out an Internet cafe where they could try and get word to Minh. It had been so long since they had disappeared that the Clan were probably not monitoring his correspondence any longer. But it seemed wisest not to take the chance.

Instead, they reverted to their backup plan. This was a relatively simple trick, which was almost untraceable. Minh had set up a website that claimed to be selling upgrade parts for computers. Actually, the website was a fake, with prices so high and equipment so outdated that no-one else would ever actually buy off it.

Sinter logged in, and went through the procedure to make a purchase, buying a particular kind of hard drive. As soon as the purchase was made, an email would be sent to Minh. To anyone monitoring his communications, it would not appear suspicious. Minh, though, would know it was a signal, that it meant his network was compromised. When he received the signal he knew to take himself somewhere far from home, where he knew he was not being watched, before contacting Saker and Sinter.

They sat in the Internet cafe for two hours after sending the email, pretending to be browsing the web, before a picture popped up. It was a live video feed from Minh in Vietnam. He was wearing a headset, sitting looking into a webcam, and behind him they could see what appeared to be a public gamer's cafe.

"I can't believe you've made me come out here," Minh complained. "I hate these places, none of these people know anything about technology. They've got enough processing power to land a rocket on Jupiter, but they act as if it was made so they can shoot pretend aliens!"

Saker's jaw practically hit the floor. "Minh, you are absolutely unbelievable!" he started. "We haven't spoken to you for months, we even thought each other was dead, and you're moaning about having to step outside your house for a few minutes!"

"What do you mean out of contact?" Minh snorted. "I had an email from you last week. In fact you're kind enough to send one about once a fortnight, telling me about all the lovely places you're visiting, spending all our money. The reason I don't respond is that a third of that money should be mine, and if you're not going to save the world or whatever, then you should give it to me, so I can at least upgrade all my machines!"

Saker and Sinter stared at each other in disbelief, then Sinter spoke. "Minh, listen to me. We have been on the Arctic tundra with no comms whatsoever until this morning. Whoever has been sending you messages, it is not us. The reason we've used our back-up plan is because your network has been compromised. Minh, they think we're dead, and they're pretending to be us, playing you along, keeping tabs on everything you're doing."

Minh's eyes dropped. For a second they thought he might apologise, or ask how they were. However, his brain really wasn't wired that way.

"I told you my firewalls needed upgrading. If you'd have let me get the servers I asked for, I'd be spying on *them* by now."

Saker threw his eyes to the heavens, but Sinter butted in, anxious that they shouldn't offend Minh. He was important to them.

"Minh, you can use our fund to get whatever you need, I'm sorry we left you underpowered. How long do you need?"

"To get secure?" Minh was practically salivating now, thinking of all the equipment he could buy. "Well I'll have to start from scratch, but leave all the existing systems running so whoever's tracking me doesn't get suspicious. A week I guess?"

"OK," Sinter answered. "Whatever it takes. But then

this is the hard bit. We failed with Hep Rylander. We haven't managed to stop what's going on with the wolves, or in the Yamal, but the scale of their operations here is even bigger than we realised. They're already shipping out oil by the truckload, and their pipeline is operational. Is there anything you can do?"

Minh smiled, and flicked the hair out of his eyes. "As it happens, I do have a plan. I'll let you know more when I speak to you next. By then I'll have a machine even the Pentagon couldn't hack."

With that, his dialogue box closed, and he logged off.

"I've never seen him smile before," Saker said.

"If only we'd known all we needed to do was buy him a new hard drive," Sinter replied. "What do you think his big plan is?"

"No idea," Saker shook his head. "But until we do, we need to lie low."

That was to prove harder than either of them had imagined. It was quite a big city, with two hundred thousand inhabitants, but the two were as conspicuous as if they had been riding around on the back of a giant seahorse! Indian skin was rarely if ever seen, and people would stop and openly stare at Sinter in the street. It didn't take long before they decided merely to take up residence in a grotty bed and breakfast, and that Saker would go out for food, which he would bring back. It seemed the longest week of their lives, but finally it was done, and they made their way back to the Internet cafe.

This time, as soon as they logged in, Minh's face popped up on the screen. Now he was back in his own home, surrounded by banks and banks of new machines in graphite-grey titanium cases. He looked immensely smug.

"Are you sure this is safe, Minh?" Saker asked concerned.

A look of panic crossed Minh's face. "I'm not sure . . . hang on, we're being traced, is that, I think someone's coming in at the door!"

Saker and Sinter nearly jumped out of their seats. But then found themselves staring at Minh's even smugger face.

"What do you take me for?" he said, his voice laced with sarcasm. "Every single thing I say is broken down by algorithms into several hundred lines of code, each line of which is bounced around the world through about a thousand different servers before it gets to you, and then the same on the way back. I am unhackable. No-one can hack me. And if they try, I'll hack them back, I'll hack them senseless."

"Well done, Minh," Sinter enthused. "There really is no-one who can beat you at this stuff."

Saker tutted. Perfect, all Minh needed was more ego!

"Did you find who's been watching you then?" Saker asked. "And who's been pretending to be us?" He didn't really expect to get an answer. He'd only really asked in order to remind Minh of his recent failures, to try and take the shine off Minh's self-importance. So Minh's reply caught him totally off guard.

"Of course," Minh responded. "That was the first thing I did."

After looking over their shoulders to check no-one was eavesdropping, both Saker and Sinter leaned in to the screen with expectation.

"They're quite advanced," Minh continued. "Well-funded. Luckily I still have the old system running, and they don't know that I've sussed them out. I just had to attach locator signal worms to an email to them. They're sophisticated, their communiques are bounced around servers all round the planet, like mine."

"So how can you track it then?" Saker asked.

"They're not as good as me," Minh stated with certainty. "I attached several thousand of my worms. They transmit signals back, telling me where to focus my search. Most end up in dead ends, coming back from servers in Australia or Chile or something. But eventually you get clusters, patterns. By focusing on groups of signals you can get the epicentre."

"And where is it?" Saker was desperate now.

"It's a curious thing," Minh blew the hair out of his eyes. "But the epicentre is in the middle of a huge forest. It's supposed to be uninhabited, there's no power into the area. It's supposed to be a massive wilderness."

"Where is it?" said Saker.

"Poland," Minh replied, transmitting a map with a pulsating red dot showing the exact location.

Saker sat back in his chair, nodding to himself, a

troubled smile playing on his lips. Of course! It made perfect sense. In an instant he was transported back, to days spent in the primeval forests that once sprawled across the whole of Europe. All of a sudden, in his mind he was running feral with a dozen other Clan boys, their faces and chests painted with war paint, brandishing homemade spears, knives, bows and arrows . . . In his vision they started to transform into beasts, their teeth sharpen into fangs, their eyes suddenly yellow with slit-shaped pupils.

"Saker!" Sinter was shaking his leg. He leapt back into consciousness.

"What?" He snapped back into reality. "Yes. It makes perfect sense. That's right, I know. I think I've always known it. The Clan proving grounds, I know exactly where they are."

23

Lounging back in his swivel chair, Yevgeny Poliakov stretched his hands above his head and gave an exaggerated yawn. He leaned forward to the desk in front of him, and took a long swig of brandy. The military weren't supposed to drink on duty, but it was 2am, and he was on his own in the massive viewing room. All the computer terminals were lying empty, the only illumination in the room came from the huge screen, with its constantly moving image of the earth.

Yevgeny swilled the powerful alcohol round in his mouth before swallowing it. He was not paying too much attention to the satellite images on the big screen. Nothing was happening on it. Nothing ever happened. The control room was buried in a bunker deep beneath the Kremlin, and had a direct feed to all of Russia's surveillance satellites. And not just the Russians' own satellites; they had hacked access into the satellites of about twenty other nations, who were unwittingly sending them endless feeds from all over the planet.

When he had taken the job, Yevgeny had been buzzing with excitement. He was a spy! The technology allowed him to stare into the backyards of just about any person on earth, to read his next-door neighbour's car number plate from here in this dark basement! He could know everyone's business, peer over the shoulder of anyone he fancied . . . The power was intoxicating.

However, after six years of nightshifts sitting yawning while watching the same old feeds on the cameras, he had also realised it was quite astoundingly boring. After the first few years, he had already peered into the houses of the colleagues he didn't like, and it became obvious that this amount of technology was pretty pointless. After all, there was no chance that the Americans or Chinese were suddenly going to invade Russia. And if they did, they weren't going to do it the old-fashioned way.

Yevgeny was never going to suddenly discover hundreds of tanks massing on their borders, or find an evil villain stockpiling nuclear weapons. He would never be a big hero. His job, sometimes it seemed his whole life, was totally pointless.

Standing up, he wandered through the deserted desks to a computer terminal that was hooked up to the internet, and logged in to the office emails. A mail popped up from a friend, giving a link to a YouTube clip of a kitten playing with its own shadow on a wall. Yevgeny watched it three times. That was as good as the night would usually get.

But then the familiar "ping" of an email arriving made him sit up and rub his eyes. The email was marked "Confidential. For Your Eyes only". That alone was enough to excite interest, almost like a message in a bottle from another era, when spying was natural as breathing. However, it was the sender that really made the breath catch in the back of Yevgeny's gullet. Ivan Markov. Yevgeny's heart beat faster. Markov was a four-star general, a man whose words could mean life or death to thousands. In the old Soviet days, his kind completely ran one of the largest and most powerful nations on earth. They could send a dissenter to the gulags on nothing more than a whim . . .

Yevgeny looked at the email, sweat beading on his forehead. Was it a joke? One of his comrades who'd run out of funny cat clips to send and had come up with this instead? His eyes flicked nervously around the room. Standing, he checked the main door. The corridor beyond was empty and silent. He was not being watched. As if about to pick up a white-hot coal, Yevgeny's fingers dropped to the mouse, moved the cursor over the email, and opened it.

Comrade Poliakoff the mail began. Yevgeny gulped. *This is not a drill. The contents of this message are strictly confidential, and cannot be shared with anyone, even your direct superiors. We have had reports of illicit activity in the Yamal peninsula, specifically*

70 degrees north, 40 minutes and fifteen seconds. Yevgeny recognised these as latitude co-ordinates. Using emergency protocols you are required to take control of the Blackhawk geostationary satellite, and divert it to fly over the Yamal filming at full resolution. This footage must be recorded and emailed back to this address within the hour. Your nation expects you to do your duty.

The mail was signed *General Markov*.

The beading on Yevgeny's forehead had turned into a full flow of sweat, dripping off the end of his nose. To say this was highly irregular was a massive understatement. The Blackhawk satellite belonged to the Czech Republic, and was not even supposed to exist. To take control of another nation's secret spy satellite could be considered an act of war. And why would he receive this by email? Why wasn't General Markov calling him on the phone, or sending someone in person? At that second, the telephone rang. He leapt straight into the air, as if a gunshot had rung out.

Picking up the phone with shaky hand, he answered.

"Comrade Poliakoff" the curt voice said, more demanding than questioning.

"Da, yes," Yevgeny replied, unconsciously standing to attention.

"You know who this is." Again, it was a statement, not a question.

"Yes, General," Yevgeny stammered, then; "It is a tremendous honour . . . " but the voice cut him off.

"You know what is required of you. Your nation expects that you will do your duty."

Yevgeny nodded. The general's command was impossible to ignore. The voice was almost robotic, the phrases repeated as if to a script, totally assured and certain.

"What is it I am looking for, General?'

"Once you have taken the images, you will return them to me through the secure email I have provided. You will not disclose this information to anyone."

Yevgeny was puzzled, the General had not answered his question at all!

"You will know what the target is when you see it, comrade," the General continued. Yevgeny breathed more easily. "It should be obvious, even to someone of limited intelligence, and certainly for someone of your experience."

"But, General," Yevgeny stuttered. "A job like this requires clearance. I will need permission, codes, it is . . . "

Again the voice cut in, as if Yevgeny had not even spoken.

"This is a matter of imperative national security. If you complete it to my satisfaction, there will be rewards for you. We do not forget Russia's heroes."

Yevgeny started, his mind suddenly full of images of medals and plaudits.

"Of course comrade General, I know the pass-codes. I know they are supposed to be kept secret, but . . . "

"We expect the information within the hour. Do not disappoint us."

The line went dead. Yevgeny breathed out, as if he had been holding his breath for the entire conversation.

The phone call cemented in his mind that this was not a drill , and was not a joke. The telephone number of this bunker was strictly classified. You could sooner have found the number of the Russian president than that direct line. And the secure email; the Americans surely weren't sophisticated enough to hack into that? Something about the voice on the phone did trouble him though. The accent and language were perfect, but it all seemed so prepared, the voice had barely acknowledged his existence.

"I guess that is just how important people work," Yevgeny reasoned. "They don't have any thought for little people like me."

His mind was made up. He would not call his superior. If he was honest, the boss was an arrogant slob, and didn't deserve to be given any credit for this job. Yevgeny should be the one who got recognised, who got the medals. He was being given an opportunity to work on his own initiative, and he would take it. He would be a hero.

Sitting down at the main console, Yevgeny typed in his secure log in, and then his fingers started to whirr over the keyboard. This would not be a simple bit of hacking. Spy satellites simply cannot be hacked into from the outside world, no matter how talented the hacker. They could only be operated from inside their respective control centres.

Worldwide hackers were getting so good that it would be too risky otherwise. To get control of Blackhawk, Yevgeny would have to con his counterpart in the Czech Republic to alter its course and begin filming.

His plan, though, was a kind of bold genius. He would replicate exactly what had just happened to him, but as a bluff! He would get in touch with the operator in the Czech bunker, pretending to be a senior military general! Yevgeny set about his plan, feeling more and more like a proper spy with every tap on the keyboard.

Well into the early hours of the morning, no more than a short time before the other workers would start to arrive, Yevgeny lay flat out and snoring, using his keyboard as a pillow. He had worked through the night. He was woken by a series of beeps on his computer; incoming mail!

Sitting up, he wiped the sleep from his bleary eyes, and opened the first mail. It was from his counterpart in Prague. Attached was a massive movie file. He clicked "Open", and images started to beam back on the screen in front of him, images from a spy camera high high above the Yamal. Unbelievably, his counterpart in Czech Republic had swallowed the bait! Yevgeny was barely able to contain his excitement.

The camera tracked over the tundra, filming the scenery below in exquisite detail. Yevgeny controlled the cameras with a rollerball and zoom control, focusing so close that he could see the antlers on the heads of individual reindeer, see their shadows moving across the brown ground as they grazed. As he moved the cameras, he followed the progress on the official maps of the Yamal, checking for any irregularity that might be what the general was looking for. Nothing. Nothing but barren miles of empty tundra, brown and boring. Suddenly, he sat bolt upright. What was that? That wasn't supposed to be there! He searched the charts in front of him in vain. There wasn't supposed to be anything, just wilderness, certainly not what had appeared on the cameras. This was undoubtedly what the general was after. After recording as much as he could, Yevgeny packaged all the video files and forwarded them. He didn't have to wait long, before an email came back.

Comrade Yevgeny (or should I say "Major Poliakov") Yevgeny felt a fierce red blush spreading over his cheeks; Major! That was more than he had dared dream of! He read on. *You have done outstandingly well. Your efforts will be rewarded.* That was it. He read it through several times, before sitting back in his chair, hands behind his head. What a night! What a morning!

About half an hour later, the first of the day shift workers came in. It was Mikhail, a lazy boorish man whom Yevgeny detested. Much as he longed to tell him of his triumph, he knew that he could not. And besides, Mikhail was obviously bursting with his own piece of gossip.

"You are not going to believe what has happened!" he puffed. "All hell has broken loose, the Kremlin is going crazy!"

Yevgeny smiled to himself. Oh yes, he knew about that all right!

"Someone has hacked into a foreign weather satellite and flown it over the Yamal!" Mikhail continued. Yevgeny's heart stopped beating. His blood seemed to run cold in his veins.

"And worse than that, they recorded everything, and posted it on the internet, it's all over YouTube! Someone is definitely going to the gulags for this!"

Yevgeny didn't say a word. He just ran to the internet and brought up YouTube. He didn't even need to type in a search. There it was on the opening page; "Satellites reveal RAM corp drilling illegally for oil in the Arctic refuge".

Alongside it, the amount of views was already past two million, and flying upwards second by second. With dread rising in the back of his throat, Yevgeny clicked on it, but he already knew what he was going to see.

It was his own footage, exactly as he had recorded it, but overlaid on the satellite pictures were graphics stating what everything shown in the video actually represented. There he saw the vast dead straight line of the mighty thousand mile pipeline. A box popped up alongside it, detailing that the pipeline was not supposed to exist, that is should not have been built for at least three years to allow the eco studies to be completed. And there, a huge refinery the size of a city, in the midst of a protected Arctic refuge, again not yet supposed to exist. The cameras zoomed out to reveal the brown stain across the landscape downwind of the cooling towers, where acid rain had destroyed the trees, the sludge of pollution in what should have been clear Arctic streams.

It was all Yevgeny could do not to be physically sick. It was obvious what had happened. Someone had tricked him. A hacker of phenomenal skill, who knew he could not operate the satellites from outside the bunker. The hacker had found his email, and telephone number. And that explained why the General's voice had been so one-sided and sounded so robotic; it was a pre-recorded, computer translation. Yevgeny had been trying to have a conversation with a machine!

"You look as though someone has walked on your grave," joked Mikhail. "Whoever is responsible for this will never see sunlight again!" So typical of his colleague to take such glee in another's misfortune. What was he going to do? And then, he had another brainwave.

"Mikhail," he said. "It has been a very boring night for me. Will you do me a favour and get me a coffee? I will pay for one for you as well." Mikhail looked at him suspiciously.

"I'll throw in one of those lard buns you like so much," Yevgeny offered. The smile instantly returned to Mikhail's face. He took the proffered ruble note, and left the room in search of sticky buns.

Time was now everything. Yevgeny scampered around the command centre, deleting everything; emails, video files, web history and searches. He hid the maps, shredded the print outs, and even wiped the phone and rollerball free of his fingerprints. There could be no trace of his stupidity. He had told no-one, so no-one knew. As long as he never spoke of it again to anyone, somebody else could take the blame.

Just as the last email was erased and the trash emptied, Mikhail came back in, cheeks stuffed with bun. "You should go home, it must have been a long night."

Yevgeny nodded. Mikhail had no idea.

24

It had been a lousy night for Hep Rylander too. Much as he hated to be back in the Yamal, there was so much to be done, and he didn't trust anyone else with the work. Even the silk sheets on his vast four-poster bed couldn't make him feel at home, or help him sleep any better. There was something about this place in the wilderness that was just so . . . backward. So depressing. He didn't understand how anyone could put up with it for more than a few days.

In an all-fired up hurry to get things done as soon as humanly possible; "So I don't have to come back to this sewer of a place no more," Rylander had intensified work on the pipeline and instructed exploratory drilling just off-shore.

His new Texan foreman was extremely concerned. "It's a marine reserve, boss," he said. "It's totally illegal to drill there. You'll catch all kinds of hell if anyone finds out."

"Who's going to care?" Hep responded. "This place is good for nothing, and I'm making it worth something. They should give me a medal!"

"If any of you mention eco-this and environment-that one more time, I'm going to have you out on the pipeline fixing rusty bolts till the day you die!"

As usual, his words had sent them scampering off with their tails firmly between their legs. The lanky Texan foreman, though, had stayed a little longer. Certainly long enough to treat Hep to a single raised eyebrow that said; "Don't push this too far or you could regret it."

Things had got even worse for Hep when he went to collect his cargo of wolf skins, ready for shipment to the Middle East. He'd been met by Sergei, who had transformed from the apologetic and cowed foreman he once was. He was practically glowing, and so manic that Hep's instant thought was that he had been drinking a little too much vodka.

"So what you got for me, Vladmir?" Hep asked, deliberately getting Sergei's name wrong. "Right now I ain't seeing nothing, and nothing don't pay the bills, son!"

"There is nothing," Sergei replied, almost breathless. "There is nothing to give you, not today, not ever. The wolves are watching us, and they have a shadow to protect them."

Hep had seen the fervour of mania before. He'd seen

men driven crazy by the lure of oil, the black gold. He'd seen preachers in his native Texas so filled with passion that they allowed themselves to be bitten by rattlesnakes, believing their god would save them. They had the same, glassy-eyed nervous energy that he saw before him right now, and he wasn't going to stand for it.

"I don't know what's wrong with you, but you just swallowed a whole bucket load of crazy. Now you start talking some sense, or I'm going to give you something to get really excited about!"

Sergei leaned towards Hep like a conspirator; "The Shadow," he whispered.

Rylander wrinkled his nose at the smell of stale breath.

"The Shadow is watching us." Sergei looked over both shoulders. "He sees our sins, and he is punishing us."

"I've had just about a skinful of your cockaninny nonsense, Vladimir," Hep retorted, pushing him away. "Now you tell me where my darn skins is at, and then you consider yourself good 'n fired. No benefits, no marching order pay off. Hell you can even give your boots back before you leave, on your way to the mentalists convention!"

"It doesn't matter," Sergei hissed. "It doesn't matter what you say to me, only The Shadow matters. And he's watching you!"

"Who in tarnation is the Shadow?!" Hep asked in exasperation. Sergei stiffened, then leaned back in, fixing Hep with his scary, manic eyes.

"The Shadow is man, and he is a ghost, but most of all, he is a wolf!"

Hep had wasted no time in sacking Sergei from the hunting party, but there was no escaping the fact that all his hunters seemed to be infected with Sergei's same brand of crazy and were refusing to go out and trap. Had the whole world gone mad?

Back in his apartment, Hep pulled on his pyjamas, and took a chilled bottle of vintage French wine from the fridge. He pulled back the sheets on his bed, lay down and poured himself a glass. The stuffed polar bear loomed ominously (if faintly ridiculously). Hep raised his wine glass in toast.

"The whole world's gone plain froot loops, Mr Bear. Only sane one's you and me, and you're stuffed full of wool, and got M&Ms for eyeballs."

There was a banging at the door. Who on earth could that be? The banging continued and then, unbelievably, the door "shushed" open and he heard boots on his granite tiled floor.

"What in Sam Hill is going on?" he demanded indignantly, as his foreman strode into the room. The Texan foreman usually had the same all-year-round tan as Hep himself, but his face was ashen.

Hep, on the other hand, looked as if he was about to burst a blood vessel. "Son, you'd better be bringing in good news, 'cos I'm all out of Mr Nice right now," Hep thundered.

"I'm afraid not, sir," the foreman responded, looking

at the floor. "You need to look at this." He opened a laptop and passed it to his boss. Hep took the computer and looked at the images flashing in front of him.

"What the heckfire is this?" he demanded. "Some kind of dumb video game?"

"That is us, sir," the foreman replied. "It's the Yamal seen from a satellite. Those are our pipelines, our refinery, our pollution, none of which is supposed to be here. In other words sir, this is the end."

"You're breaking my heart boy, what has this got to do with the price of crude?"

"Sir . . . those images are currently spanning the world. Over three million views so far. And if every kid from Kansas to Constantinople has seen them, you can bet the senators, and the Kremlin, and, well, everyone else has seen them too."

Hep sat down as if the bones had disappeared from his legs. He looked at the images again, still not understanding what they meant.

"But this is all kinds of crazy," he muttered. "There's nothing out here, everyone knows that. Nothing but blackfly and blizzards, and a few savages wrapped in seal skin and eating yellow snowballs. I'm bringing something to nothing, I'm making this place worth money, I'm . . . I'm . . . Heck, I'm just a middleman. Do you have any idea how many important people had to know about this? It's not just me. They all know, every one of them got kickbacks, they're getting rich off this too."

"They may know," the foreman replied. "But they can't be seen to know. You've broken every single environmental law there is. And that was fine while nobody knew . . . "

"Environ-mental! Don't you say that word to me ever again, boy!" Hep was still fighting. "They can't hang me out to dry for this, I have proof, I ain't going down alone. They can't keep me quiet." Hep was desperate now. "If I'm going to pay, they're all going to pay!"

His rant was cut short by a low frequency whirring sound. Hep jumped to his feet, and ran to the huge plate glass windows, his pyjamas flapping around his ankles. Tearing back the curtains, he revealed the tundra beyond. There, in an ominous line, approaching like vast black hovering dung beetles were four huge Chinook helicopters, bearing down on the plant with a menacing inevitability. They may as well have been the horsemen of the Apocalypse.

Hep's face drained of all colour. "We have to notify the press NOW!" he shouted. "Get me my sat phone!"

But as he turned he saw his foreman flanked by two Russian henchmen. All three wore grim smiles.

"I'm real sorry," the foreman said, taking a pair of handcuffs from his pocket and walking forward. "I guess what goes around comes around."

25

On a high cliff edge, with a dizzying drop overlooking a barren dry valley flanked with grey peaks, a boy sat whittling a small piece of kindling in his hands. Bearded vultures circled below him, looking for broken bodies to pick clean, in order to drop the bones from high and smash them apart. The boy stood holding the wooden carving in his fingers, turning it to appreciate it from all angles. Something about its symmetry displeased him, and he threw the offending amulet into the void, before sitting back down, and taking up a fresh piece of wood.

Shaping and carving wooden bullets had become habit for Saker, like worry beads, or a monk who never stops doing his rosary. He polished every single one as if it was some kind of holy artefact. Sometimes Sinter feared he'd wear the wood clean away with his efforts.

She often meant to go up to him in his isolated eyrie,

to try and talk to him about his obsession, to tell him she was worried about him. Something told her it would be a waste of time. There was also a lot to be said for Saker burying himself in simple mindless tasks. So much had happened in the last few weeks that it was almost impossible to catch breath, let alone make sense of it all.

Minh's plan had been triumphant. Hacking into the command centre and conning them into using spy satellites had been genius, but had left Saker with no role to play. He felt useless. Sinter had rejoiced at Hep Rylander's very public unveiling, at the international incident it had sparked, at the ending of all drilling in the Yamal until proper surveys could take place. Saker on the other hand had just felt more and more redundant.

But it wasn't powerlessness that was dominating his thoughts, far from it. Saker now knew exactly where the Clan was based. The location of the proving grounds in the ancient forests of Poland was kept strictly secret. Even the initiates of the Clan had no idea where they were. The boys would be transported in and out of the forest in trucks with blacked-out windows, and it had been very clear that trying to find out where the hub was would result in terrible punishment.

Now, thanks to Minh's computer worms, hacking then tracking the Clan spyware that was supposed to be spying on him, Minh could pinpoint the Clan's position to within a matter of miles.

If it had been down to Sinter, then the obvious course

of action would be to use this information to get as far away as possible. But Saker had a much more confrontational nature. His instant reaction was to arm himself to the hilt, and storm into the forest all guns blazing, killing the Prophet, Wolf and anyone else who got in his way.

"The best form of defence is attack," he told Sinter. "I need to do it now, while they're least expecting it."

"That's the sort of thing action stars say in the movies," she replied. "It's not actually true! Think about it, if you go storming into the Clan grounds, where they're strongest, you'll be taking on the whole Clan. Alone.

"You can't possibly win. They'll take you, and you'll never be seen alive. Either that or you'll be reprogrammed and sent back out to do awful things again." She rubbed the back of her hand. The Prophet had once injected her with drugs that had taken over her mind, and made her do terrible things she did not want to do. The needles had left small scars on her flesh, but much bigger ones in her mind.

Sinter too had demons to battle with. It seemed every fresh day brought not answers but more questions, and she was still no wiser about what their next course of action should be. She was also bearing the burden of her thoughts and theories on the origins of the Clan. She hadn't said a word to Saker about her theory that scientists could have been manipulating the boys DNA, tampering with their abilities, giving them superhuman skills by blending their genes with those of predators.

There hadn't been a time when it seemed right to bring it up! What was she going to say? "By the way Saker, you know you never knew your mother? Well, I reckon you might actually have been born half man, half falcon!"

But though she kept it to herself, she had become more and more convinced with each passing day. Every time Saker's head bobbed as if searching for focus, every time his head snapped round a little too fast in reaction to a sound she couldn't hear, or sight she couldn't see. Every time, Sinter looked at her friend, and thought; "It's obvious, how can I have been so blind?"

By now they had made their way many miles south from the Yamal, crossing out of Russia, and into the mountains of Kazakhstan. Here they had made camp with a group of Kazakh nomads, who lived their whole life on horseback, hunting animals like foxes and mountain goats using trained golden eagles, which they kept on huge gauntlets on their wrists. The Kazakhs had a dignity and regal bearing that both Saker and Sinter found impressive. And just like the Nenet they took the pair in to their camps without question or request for payment. Not for the first time, Sinter had cause to reflect on how people living simple lives appeared so much nicer, so much friendlier than those in big cities who had everything.

In response to his role becoming less and less important, Saker decided to get more and more physical. If he wasn't carving bullets, he would be training. Every day, he would run for many miles through the rugged, dry, rocky peaks. In the morning he would meditate and do yoga before sunrise, before brutal martial arts training that bordered on the psychotic. He would take a single move, and do it a thousand times, practising it until it had become as natural as breathing. To harden the bones in his fists and shins, and deaden the nerve endings so kicks and punches would no longer hurt, he beat his lower legs with heavy glass bottles, punched rocks over and over again, and did press ups on his knuckles until the skin bled.

Raising his feet on wooden blocks, he would hold his whole body in the splits. Hands clasped in front of him, eyes closed, he'd focus on his breathing, until the pain was so overwhelming that he'd collapse, sobbing with relief and agony. It was obvious that he was preparing himself for a showdown. Sinter hoped more than anything that he would see sense, but deep down she knew that would never happen.

Eventually, one morning she walked into his tent to find him packing his one small bag with everything he owned.

"You're leaving," she said simply. It was a statement, not a question.

"I figure I can get the jump on them now, get ahead of the game, you know how it is."

"Yes," she replied. "I know how it is." She sat down on his wooden camp bed, and watched as he meticulously folded his clothes.

"What is it you're trying to find, Saker?" she asked. He stopped what he was doing, and looked down at his feet.

"I know that you have lost everything you had," he began. "That your mother is gone, that your father betrayed you, that you have no home . . ."

"I have you!" she interrupted, but Saker held up his hand to show he had not finished.

"But at least you *know*," he said. "At least you know where you come from. At least you know who you are. I don't know anything at all. All I have is a few shady memories, and nightmares, which get weirder, and further from reality every single day. I need to know who I am. That's all."

Sinter sighed. If she didn't bring it up now, then perhaps she never would. "Saker. Have you got any idea of where the Clan boys come from? Of why you can do the things you can do?"

Saker studied her. "I always figured we were kidnapped. Stolen from our mothers. Somewhere out there is a family without a son, and whether they want me or not, I need to find out."

Sinter nodded cautiously. " So how do they get away with it? Why hasn't anyone stopped them?"

Saker shrugged. "I dunno. They just do. And then they train us from birth. It's not surprising we're the best."

"But you're so like your totem animals. Didn't you ever wonder about that?"

Saker shook his head. "No . . . Well, it's so obvious. I

mean, the falcon, it's like a part of me. I'm . . . I *am* a falcon, I guess. I've spent so many years being trained like one that I've sort of become one."

"Did anyone ever grow up not like their totem animal? I mean was anyone ever given the name mamba, and then grew up to be more of a marmoset? Does that not seem odd?"

"No," he was puzzled now. "We just are like that. We . . . I . . . what are you getting at?"

She breathed out. Here it was. "I'm wondering, I'm thinking perhaps that . . . I don't know, maybe you were mixed with a Saker Falcon. That maybe you feel half falcon, because you are. Because somewhere along the line someone actually mixed you with a bit of falcon." She stopped. Perhaps that was too much.

"What are you saying?" Saker replied in horror. "That I'm some kind of a freak? That I'm an experiment gone wrong? Just because I can do things you can't doesn't make me a monster!"

"No, no, of course not," she began, but was instantly cut off.

"You'll never understand," Saker said. "No-one who didn't grow up there could ever understand. And that's why I have to go back."

"Stop," she implored. "Saker stop, please, we've only just found each other. I can't lose you again already!"

Saker did indeed stop, and walked slowly back over to his friend, taking her face in his hands. "When I was in that place, in the ice cave," Sinter nodded, she knew what he meant. "I couldn't stop myself thinking about you, about the fact that you were gone. I've never . . . well, I've never felt that way about anyone before."

Sinter nodded again, tears had started to pour down her cheeks.

" You are like . . ." he fought for the words. Like a sister? No, that didn't seem quite right. "You are so special to me, you're all I have."

"And you're all I have too Saker. For goodness sake stop being so stubborn."

"But that is why I have to do this," he said. "Unless I solve it, they will always be hunting us. Be hunting you. And until I know who I really am, I cannot be . . ."

He looked down at her tear-streaked face, seeking the right words. "I cannot be a true friend to you. I will always be wondering."

Sinter's eyes dropped, and she nodded her head. Saker bent and kissed her once on the forehead, and then was gone.

EPILOGUE

A utumn had come to the forest. They call it "Fall"
in America, for it is the time when trees take their
life-giving chlorophyll from their leaves, and
those leaves fall to the ground, charred brown boats drifting
on the currents of the breeze. The trees burn with reds,
toasted yellows and golds too glorious for words, before
the bleakness of winter sets in.

The glade below the dazzling colours is filled with a
spectacle of its own, but a secret one. Here, a quadrant
of twenty boys with close-cropped hair, clad in light grey
karate suits, is engaged in martial arts training. At the front
of the group stands an imposing figure. He wears the loose-
fitting blue robe of a Japanese samurai, his clipped shaven
hair pure white against his scalp. His eyes the blue of
glacial ice.

As the Prophet performs each manoeuvre, he drives
the air out of his lungs, concentrating all of his force into

each strike, crying out in a furious bellow. The students repeat his gestures exactly, then mimic his yells. The normal forest sounds of birdsong and wind chiming through leaves are overwhelmed by the echoes of the unfamiliar sounds. The clatter of quarterstaff poles as the Clan boys begin their weapons training, howls of pain as some boys take a pounding and whoops of triumph from those who are doing the beating. Among them all the Prophet strides, hands behind his back, watching his charges like a farmer might stride among his prize bulls just before they're sent to market.

Suddenly, another boy approaches the Prophet. He is older, not dressed for combat training, but clearly comes with purpose. Calling for the Prophet's favour, he whispers into his ear. The Prophet's eyes narrow. Something extraordinary has happened. Now the roar of simulated battle is a disturbance. "Mattay!" he calls in irritation; "Cease!"

The sweating warriors abruptly stop, take up their quadrant formation, and stand facing the front, chests heaving as they try to regain their breath. The Prophet addresses the older boy; " Explain yourself."

"He's not dead", the boy says. "He didn't die in the snow as we believed, he is still alive."

The white-haired man scratches his ivory-stained scalp. "I have been misinformed," he says. "Misinformed, or perhaps lied to." His tone is as clipped as his hair.

"We don't know how he survived the avalanche, but

the girl must surely be gone," the boy continues. "He is alone."

"How so?"

The man's questions are abrupt. There is an undercurrent that says; "Lie to me, and I will line your grave with rose petals."

"There are tales from Russia, and reports from the borders. A lone boy, a shadow. Until now it was merely rumour, but there is now no doubt. And it looks more and more likely that he had a hand in the oil deal going down. Perhaps his hacker contact in Vietnam."

The Prophet strokes his head once more. "Arrangements must be made. No more loose ends, no second chances. This time there will be no excuses, no escape. This time the falcon will meet the falconer."

The boy nods and runs off. The Prophet straightens his light blue Samurai jacket, and walks to the rack of weapons that stands beneath a towering beech tree. Taking his time, he chooses a samurai sword in a lacquered black and red scabbard and takes it into his hands. Holding it at shoulder height, and parallel to the ground, he slides the sheath and the braided handle apart. It reveals the blade, tempered steel, folded thousands of times in the sharpening process, the cutting edge so keen that flesh seems to leap apart at its very whisper.

The Prophet studies the blade. His own blue eyes stare back at him from the steel.

AUTHOR'S NOTE

I remember the first time I saw a wild wolf, with a piercing clarity matched only by the eyes of the wolf itself. I was totally unprepared for it. Granted, my family have always been dog crazy, and never had one far from the hearth, but when it came to wild animals, I was always more into snakes and spiders than furry stuff. That first wolf changed everything. If I try to think about it intellectually, it's their beauty, the fact that they have such complex pack structures, that they communicate, play, love, fight and even grieve.

But that isn't it at all. It's more akin to that chill that surges up the nape of your neck when you hear a wolf howl on a moonlit night. In his *A Dance with Dragons* George R Martin wrote; *A man might befriend a wolf, even break a wolf, but no man could truly tame a wolf.*

That is what I find so intoxicating. The wolf IS the wilderness. It is the primal parts of our consciousness and our world that I most want to explore. Unfortunately, this has also been the wolf's downfall. The unknown and ancient part of nature that I find most exciting is to some people just plain frightening. This has led to extraordinary persecution of wolves. They once ranged over most of the north of our planet, but are now near impossible to see anywhere. Despite the fact that they are so rare, they are still persecuted wherever they are found, most of which is due to sheer ignorance.

That first wolf changed my life. Since then I have on occasion thrown back my head and howled, and had wild wolves return the call. My fond hope is my readers might experience a little of that wonder through these pages.

It took a lot of restraint for me to write a book based in the Arctic and not theme it on climate change. The human-induced climate change that we, in our centrally-heated houses hear on the news, tut and argue about, can be felt, touched and seen in the Arctic. Every year the polar world changes. Sea ice melts a little earlier, polar bears come into villages starving hungry as they can no longer hunt seals on the ice. Glaciers that have calved into the sea for thousands of years have retreated so far that suddenly they come to an end on land. Tundra that should be permafrost all year round is melting, releasing methane and other carbon gases into the atmosphere.

Climate change is real, we are causing it, and its effects are tangible way up north. If you hear a scientist saying otherwise, look carefully at who is sponsoring their research.

I did a lot of research into natural toxins when putting together my book Venom in 2006. Tetrodotoxin does exist; as a poison in the flesh and vital organs of pufferfish, and a venom in animals like the blue-ringed octopus. It works much as I describe, and though there is no antidote, victims HAVE been saved from its effects by being ventilated or given CPR for 24 hours until the poison leaves their system.

In addition, people HAVE seemed to be killed by extreme cold, showing no vital signs, only to come "back to life" when they are brought back to civilisation. Anne Bagenholm is a famous example; the Swedish skier was trapped under ice in freezing water for eighty minutes. Her body temperature dropped to 13 degrees C (anything under 35 is hypothermic, and often fatal) her circulation totally stopped, and she appeared dead, yet she was rewarmed and made a complete recovery. A person truly is not dead, until they are warm and dead! Sinter surviving the effects of tetrodotoxin because cold put her into a kind of hibernation is an invention of mine. It has never to my knowledge happened, but could conceivably work; the human body is a resilient thing!

It's true that snow is a great insulator, and that huskies and other Arctic beasts merely bury themselves under it to sleep. In a survival situation you're better off out of the wind and covered in a snow blanket. However, you wouldn't get a good night's sleep, or any sleep at all. Trust me, I've tried it; I didn't last long.

Much of the talk about wolf and dog behaviour is based on genuine ethology (the science of animal behaviour). The Nenet tale of the dog and wolf is from Jean de la Fontaine's Fables. The old hunter's tale is from a piece by Aldo Leopold.

A recurrent theme in the book is inspired by Terry Pratchett, who wrote; *There are some dogs which, when you meet them, remind you that, despite thousands of years of manmade evolution, every dog is still only two meals away from being a wolf. These dogs advance deliberately, purposefully, the wilderness made flesh, their teeth yellow, their breath stink, while in the distance their owners witter, "He's an old soppy really, just poke him if he's a nuisance," and in the green of their eyes the red campfires of the Pleistocene gleam and flicker.*

I love that image, and I'm sure many of you will have met dogs just like that; though it seems far-fetched when you look at modern lapdogs and Labradors! It is, however, totally true that modern science places EVERY breed of dog as a subspecies of wolf. Many of the things they do start to make a lot of sense when you get to know their wonderful wild ancestors.

I thought long and hard about having Yantar rescue Saker from the crevasse. It seems far-fetched; like something that would have happened in a "Lassie" movie when I was a kid, which I would scoff about now. However, it is nothing to some of the heroic achievements of dogs over the years. I hope you don't find it too much of a stretch.

Much of my descriptions of sled-dogging come from

the chances I've had to run with the dogs. That and Jack London's *Call of the Wild*; my favourite book as a boy. If you enjoy this book, read *Call of the Wild*. If you hate this book read *Call of the Wild*. If you are indifferent to it . . . well, you get the message!

The talk of survivalists owes much to the works of some of the great survivors. Joe Simpson in his epic *Touching the Void* talks about how *when you are finished, you are only fifty percent done*. That same truth is found on every page of Shackleton's *South*, perhaps the greatest single book about human fortitude.

In the crevasse, Saker is given guidance by a phantom, who helps save his life. Many adventurers have talked about "the third man" on an expedition, who seems to be there giving advice. Psychologists say this is something called "displacement", a way that born survivors have of removing emotion from their decisions, subconsciously getting an imaginary third person to do it for them.

Certainly the most awe-inspiring expedition companions I've had the privilege to work with have the ability to get more calm as things get more desperate. In Kipling's words, they can *keep their heads, when all about are losing theirs and blaming it on you*. I've experienced the phantom on a few mountaineering and desert expeditions when I've felt at death's door, but I think it was probably hallucinations from not having slept in days!

The Yamal peninsula, Nenet peoples and the effects of searching for oil in the peninsula are all real. All the animals and effects of Arctic conditions are ones I have seen with my eyes and felt in my fingertips. In 2007, a baby mammoth carcass was revealed beneath the snow in the Yamal peninsula. The news story was what first excited my interest in the place. Much as in my description, the carcass looked as if it had merely laid down to sleep that very morning, despite being at least thirty seven thousand years old.

Sadly, much of what I've written about oil and gas is also true. The Yamal area is being ruthlessly drilled, with scant regard for terrain that may never recover.

Steve Backshall
Svalbard (deep inside the Arctic Circle)
September 2013

Don't miss

**SAKER AND SINTER'S
NEXT ADVENTURE**

SHARK SEAS

Here is a preview of the opening.

The Aeroflot plane taxied slowly down the runway, getting to the point where it could fire up the engines ready for take-off. Beyond the windows, and outside the chain link fence that surrounded the airport, was another grey, dull, depressing city. He was glad to be leaving. In a weird way, he was going home. In front of Saker the air hostess went through the motions she had clearly done a thousand times before; "The exits are here, here and here."

She looked so glassy-eyed bored that Saker had a mind to start making silly faces at her, or to punch out the plane windows, just to see what she'd do. Anything to get her to stop her robotic performance.

There was another reason he wanted to punch the window out. It had been a long time since he'd been on a plane. The last time, the walls of the thin metal tube had seemed to close in around him, closing in like some crazed torture method an arch-villain would use to squeeze James Bond to death. The only difference being that everyone knows Bond will escape. Saker, though, would have to endure many hours inside that metal tube, totally unable to affect his own plight. If the wings fell off, or the engines caught fire, he would just have to sit there, surrounded by screaming passengers, and let some pilot he had never even met take care of things. The one thing Saker hated more than enclosed spaces was not being in control of his own fate.

A little tap on his arm, he looked around. Beside him was a wrinkled walnut of a woman, stooped and tiny. She was grinning, and said something to him in a language he didn't understand. It was clear she was saying something comforting to help him relax and calm down. She smiled encouragingly and offered him a packet of gum. He took a stick and pushed it into his mouth, clenching and unclenching his jaw, the veins standing out on his temples. Gripping the armrests much too tight, he felt a trickle of sweat slide down the side of his cheek. He tried to smile and nod to the beaming old lady, but the tension contorted his features, so he just managed to bare his teeth like a snarling ferret. The smile disappeared from her face, and she sat back in her seat.

First his tormented mind swirled with images of the cave in Borneo, the sinkhole where he had nearly perished, locked in total darkness under a duvet of slithering and wriggling horror show beasts. But then it got even worse.

Now he had the terrors of the ice cave to torment him. A breath, and Saker was there again, frozen up to the waist in age-old ice. A vast polar bear was pounding on the thick ice-door of the cavern, its yellow-stained teeth dribbling saliva like melting icicles. The hairs stood up on his arms and his skin bubbled with gooseflesh. "Saker . . ." the phantom whispered.

"NO!" he screamed, and came to, inside the plane. The old woman alongside him withdrew in alarm.

The claustrophobia was too much. The walls were closing around him. The flight attendant was chiming her instructions like a crazed automaton, all red lip gloss and empty eyes. The seat belt signs "bonged" too loud, flashing like the wheels on a fruit machine. Saker screamed in terror and started ripping at his seatbelt, his fingers suddenly useless, frostbitten to ice lollies, incapable of even the tiniest movement. Finally getting the buckle free, he leapt to his feet. There were squeals of concern from the passengers around him. The plane was mid take-off, they were all supposed to be in their seats.

"I can't be here!" he screamed. "We need to turn the plane around!"

The tannoy started shouting angry commands in Russian, "bing bong"-ing for all it was worth. If Saker had wanted to do something to attract the bored stewardess's attention, this was it! She was out of her seat like a shot, urging him to sit down, shouting at him with words he didn't understand.

"No!" He yelled yet again. "The Phantom is here! You can't lock me away, I have to get out!"

A burly passenger now stood, rocked by the pitch and roll of the plane mid take-off. He stood a full head taller than Saker, and looked like a man who could take care of himself. He grabbed Saker by the arm and twisted, trying to put Saker into an arm lock. Even in his feverish state, Saker's training took over. Moves practised a thousand times had become as natural as taking a breath. He slipped his wrist and kept on twisting, turning the big man's arm lock against him. The man squealed in pain. Saker dropped one knee, turned and kept twisting his wrist. The big man was tossed in a neat somersault clean down the narrow aisle, and came down with a thump on his back.

The stewardess was screaming, her voice piercing through him like a too-close siren, like the wind cutting through their midnight snow cave. Saker turned, he had to shut off that terrible sound. But just as he raised his hands against her, a juddering force took control of his limbs, making him leap and jump like a puppet in the hands of an over-eager child. Looking down, Saker saw protruding from his chest two needles, attached to long wires. The rest of his body was not paying any attention to his commands. Ferocious pain seethed through every tendon, tensing his muscles, setting his teeth into a furious chattering. His eyes could still move, and followed the wires to their source. A man in a dark suit, holding what looked like a gun; the wires ran out of it. A Taser! He'd been tasered! Right now 50,000 volts were pulsing through his body. Not even the toughest or biggest of men can do anything in the face of that much force. Saker fought it with every sinew, but his whole body was bucking like a rodeo bull.

The darkness descended, strength left his limbs and he hit the floor in between the seats. The last thing he noted before losing consciousness was that the blue carpet was a thick wiry weave, and he was aware of it squishing beneath the black leather shoes of the man who had tasered him. He heard the click of the handcuffs as they closed around his wrists, and then the darkness took him.

the orion star

CALLING ALL GROWN-UPS!

Sign up for **the orion star** newsletter to
hear about your favourite authors and exclusive
competitions, plus details of how children
can join our 'Story Stars' review panel.

Sign up at:

www.orionbooks.co.uk/orionstar

Follow us 🐦 @the_orionstar
Find us 📘 facebook.com/TheOrionStar